WHAT CHANGE
MAY COME

MALA NAIDOO

Publisher: Mala Naidoo

malanaidoo.com

First Published in Australia 2019

This edition Published 2019

Copyright © Mala Naidoo 2019

Cover Design: Working Type (www.workingtype.com.au) *Cover image credits:
Caique Silva, Samuel Dixon, Saffu, Hadis-Safari, Unsplash.com*

Naidoo, Mala

What Change May Come

ISBN - 978-0-6481377-8-8

ABOUT THE AUTHOR

Mala Naidoo is an Australian author. She was born in South Africa during the apartheid era which is the impetus for her imaginative stories that take on a life of their own when the creative muse beckons. Mala believes that literature speaks through the values and culture of characters' lives, situations and choices, instilling understanding through connections to a moment in time, an event or conversation that brings clarity to daily existence.

ALSO BY MALA NAIDOO:

With Gratitude to My Loving Family

We Choose Our Joys and Sorrows Long Before We Experience Them

~ Khalil Gibran

1

THE RETURN

Separation changes the landscape of life. The strong develop cracks on the bends and twists along a rocky terrain. The entrance of newcomers and unexpected truths increase the necessity of commitment, as the old slips into the new.

When Patience returned to Sydney after almost nine months, it was not the place, but the people that were different. Had she altered during her time away, or was it as she saw it? Something had irrevocably changed in her sister Grace's life.

Three months in South Africa, then three months in an unnamed location – she believed she was traveling to Thailand, a flight deviation changed the course of her life. Thereafter a further three months in Pakistan proved intense for Patience Sharvin, head of the Sisters Helping Sisters Organisation. Her time away renewed value for the close relationship she shared with her sister, and the quiet acknowledgment that Australia was her spiritual home. The descent over Botany Bay had her peering out the window for a glimpse of dancing golden rays of sunlight, twinkling on the water's surface and across a rooftop littered landscape. She breathed deeply, closed her eyes and whispered, 'I'm home at last.'

She squashed thoughts of arriving unannounced at Grace's door, her noted act of surprise whenever she returned after a long period away. Her sister had suffered much when her flight to Thailand disappeared. They met at the airport before heading off to Brighton Bay for a leisurely water-side coffee reunion, and dinner, later, at Grace's apartment.

They hugged each other laughing and crying at the same time.

'Look at us, we've grown into sentimental old women with these uncontrolled emotions!' Patience giggled to lighten the heaviness of their joyous reunion.

'That's love for you, family love!' Grace mumbled through tears with long, black streaks of mascara staining her cheeks.

'Wipe away that panda look, Gracie! Who was watching out for you while I was away, hey sis?' Patience's husky laugh embraced what Grace needed. 'Look at you, you've wasted away while I was gone. Have you been dieting or just pining away for me?'

'No, ...not dieting... I've been walking a lot since you left. I had plenty of quiet, thinking time...' She trailed off, and then added, 'it might have been a bit of stress too, as you know. Your letters brought me relief. It gave me hope that you would return. I've started seeing Dr Deakin again for a few sessions to help me relax.'

'Oh Grace, I'm so sorry you had to endure this because of me, I'm really sorry.' Their coffee grew cold as their conversation flowed in the hurried need to reconnect.

'I feared the most when I heard you were in Pakistan on some humanitarian mission. Yet not knowing exactly where you were when your plane disappeared, brought me comfort when your letters arrived. The political situation and insensitive media coverage left me shattered, and sleepless. Enough of me, I want to know everything about your escapades.'

'You won't lie to me Grace, right? Is your health okay? You look so thin, sorry to say, anorexic really? I'm not being mean, you know that.'

'I would never lie to you about that. I'm well, trust me.' Her eyes told a different truth, clouding over in guilty hesitation. Patience accepted that Grace would only reveal anything when she was ready. Pushing her now would make her retreat in silence. She could not risk having her shut off like she did in her brush with death in South Africa.

Soon Patience caught sight of Grace's vintage diamond ring flickering in a gyrating prism of blinding colours as a shaft of sunlight caressed it.

'Hey you! You got engaged during my absence! Did you want to surprise me with the news?' Patience squealed with delight. Even as a child her joy was obvious in her vocal racket around her sister, often embarrassing Grace in public places.

'Not so loud please, I tried telling you when you were in Pakistan, during our one and only conversation from that location, but the line died on us, remember?'

'Yes, I do, and it was difficult for me to call you without telling you precisely what I was doing. Well, sister dear, congratulations! I won't be quiet about this!' She pushed her seat back, jumped up, and grabbed her sister from behind, attempting to whisper, 'I am so happy for you Grace.' She stepped back to her seat and continued with a cheeky twinkle in her eye, 'I have to ask, is it Keefe or Andrew? You, lucky fish!'

'Crazy girl! Shush! You know it can only be Keefe! Andrew is like a brother and so shall he be to the end of my days!'

'So, when will I hear wedding bells? How soon? I need to go on a diet before then, you know!' She laughed, tapping her belly, making Grace smile for a fleeting second. 'Mama Varuna and Mama Elsie would have been overjoyed with this news!'

'Yeah, coming this late in my life, it sure would have thrilled them.'

'Your Irish gentleman is a lovely man, indeed. Out with it, when's the wedding?'

'I was not going to get married without you, so that's still on hold until further notice. I need sister time now, so no wedding talk!'

The finality of Grace's words shook Patience a little. Could it be in the joy of having her back home that marriage was not up for discussion, or was there something else afoot? She stilled her *tell me now* attitude, aware that something ran deeper than her sister was prepared to reveal.

'I want to know all about this reckless adventure you've been on. I want all the details.'

'That will take a few days, but I can say, in many ways, it has been a life altering experience.'

'Really? More so than when you were abducted by the chief's henchman in South Africa?'

'Yes, for sure! It has been a social and cultural awakening.'

'You have me curious now, please don't make me wait too long.'

'I won't, I want to know all that has happened here in the last nine months. You could have had a baby in that time!' Patience laughed and stopped when she heard Grace heave a deep sigh.

She changed the direction of the conversation in response to Grace's obvious discomfort in talking about herself. 'How's Virginia doing with the Sisters Helping Sisters Organisation and taking care of Sprite and Ajax? I hope they were not troublesome. I had very few conversations with her from Pakistan given the security issues there.'

'Let Virginia tell you all about that. She has been phenomenal, and your dog-babies have been a delight, as always.'

'Has Felicity kept in touch with you while I was away?'

'She has been incredible in digging up information and

shaking up the investigation on your missing flight. She went to The Hague, rattled a few politicians and the media on their lack of interest. Sadly though, Alf is not doing too well. His health has declined considerably in recent months.'

'Oh, I'm so sorry to hear this. My contact with Felicity has been scant too. We should arrange a trip to Melbourne soon, to support her through this time. I owe you all so much for everything you've done for me.'

'Owe?' Don't be ridiculous. We pull together for the people we love, and besides you are always putting us first, not to mention your selfless care of the many women you protect from abuse.

'Thank you, Grace. I know how much you all love and care for me, but one should never exploit that. Our Mamas' instilled – never push the hand that loves and cares too far. I have done that by heading off into the unknown.'

'Nonsense! Everything in life has its own design and purpose. Dr Deakin has helped me understand that. Let's go home to my place, I have your favourite meal waiting for you.' Grace pulled her sunglasses down and peered at Patience, waiting for her response.

'Chicken curry! Like only you can cook it! You must have been up very early this morning. Will Keefe join us for dinner?'

'It gave me the greatest pleasure to prepare our homecoming meal,' she smiled, 'this is going to be *our* two days, our pyjama time together. Keefe won't be at dinner.'

Patience would not be silenced on Keefe's exclusion from dinner, more like an expulsion with Grace's tone and attitude when she spoke of him.

'I do need that alone time with you, but are you sure Keefe won't mind, now that you both are *promised* to each other?' Patience was back all right! She delighted in finding any inroad to tease Grace. Her sister's sullen disposition needed some frivolity.

'Promised? Kiss my derriere – I am never promised to anyone, you should know that!' She laughed it off, but the barb beneath her fake, reckless laugh was unmissable.

'Wow, Gracie, you're on fire, speaking with such vulgarity is *so not you!*' Patience slapped her thighs as she let out another bellowing laugh. 'It sure is good to be back in Sydney, I tell you!' Tears streamed down her cheeks, enjoying that she could relax around Grace.

'You have a knack of bringing out the real me!'

'On a serious note, it is good to be home. I have been to hell and back, but I can say I met a few angels along the way.'

AFTER A SPICY DINNER just as their mother would have cooked, and a few glasses of gin and tonic down, Patience was pumped to know more about Keefe's and Grace's love affair.

'Before I begin with my adventures, I need to know how Keefe proposed, and when did you accept. Knowing you, you would have led him on a song and dance first, Gracie!'

She explained that Keefe's mother had passed away soon after she met her in Belfast, and that Keefe's sister, Aileen, a devoted sibling, had moved to Sydney. She was in the process of setting up her legal practice. Patience listened to the shenanigans Keefe's ex-wife created before his mother's funeral.

'You've had a lot happening on your end. I'm sorry that Keefe's mum has passed on. She is in a better place, free from pain, now. The previous marriage is something Keefe revealed from the outset, right?'

'Thank you. Yes, he was upfront about the marriage.'

'So, what is it Grace? There's something you're reluctant to share. Now that's something about you that hasn't changed, it has always been difficult to get you to be open about yourself. At the risk of being a nag, I need to know what's making you tense if I am to help you.'

'You've just returned and don't need to be bothered with my

woes. Keefe's been a pillar of strength throughout the time you've been away. He advised me to see Dr Deakin again and has also encouraged me to separate my emotional and professional side to avoid overthinking when we lose a patient in ER. Things I need to be reminded about. As medics, he said, we think we are invincible and neglect to take care of our mental health.'

'Wise words, for sure, that you should heed. So, what is going on? It sounds perfect, yet looking at you, I know it's far from that.'

Grace sighed, put her left hand on her head and leaned on the table.

'Let's leave that for another day, please. I need to be with you now.'

'One question, is Keefe living here, now?'

'No, he spends the odd night, here and there.'

'I would have thought you couldn't get enough of him, and that he was part of the furniture by now!'

'Stop it! I said let's save Keefe for later. I want YOU time! I want to hear everything about your ordeal.'

'It was only an ordeal until I wrote to you. I am strong. It's you that needs care, my first task is to fatten you up!' Patience ensured that Grace was not encouraged to wallow over what she was concealing. She wanted her family back, intact as before.

'Let me tell you a bit about my time in Pakistan and tomorrow I will tell you what happened after the plane disappeared.'

Patience told Grace about Akbar and his family, and the young women at the Well Study Centre.

That night she tossed and turned in her old bed, in her sister's apartment, mulling over how the universe had conspired to cut short her time in Pakistan to get her back to Grace.

As family they had each other's backs. She would get to the bottom of what caused her sister's restless discontent. The past was a huge lesson to them both that unshared problems could lead to poor mental health. Grace's sadness baffled her.

2

SISTERS

Waking up in her old bed to the delectable smell of pancakes and brewing coffee made Patience warm and fuzzy. Sunday morning pancakes during her childhood was a much anticipated, worth the weekday wait treat. Mama Varuna added honey and a sprinkling of cinnamon with a few drops of freshly squeezed lemon for a gustatory burst of heaven! Grace was keen to indulge her sister with every mouthwatering delight she could cook to remind her of the joys of home.

Grace had some personal struggle going on but that did not deter her mothering instinct now that she was back. After a languid shower, with water cascading over her, Patience remembered her little quarter pirouette moves in the elfin shower at the Mission. Everything was better at home. Grace was a constant in her life that she would never forsake, nor take for granted. She imagined there would be a wedding soon, but where would that leave her? Would she still have the same closeness with her sister? Little did she know how soon this doubt would be played out.

Grace set up breakfast on the balcony. A beautiful, sunny

Sydney morning greeted them with the top of the Harbour Bridge peeping over in the distance. Patience donned a loose open front, cotton shirt and walked out to meet Grace. She would never be able to dress like this when Keefe was at the apartment.

'Those pancakes smell heavenly. Thank you for this treat. Did you sleep at all?'

'I knew you would relish mum's homemade pancakes and I want this to be a memorable homecoming, in the hope that you won't be up and gone again, anytime soon! Herbal sedatives are my best friends these days, so I had a deep, refreshing sleep.'

Once again Grace dropped a line to suggest her life had done a backward step while Patience was away.

'You should try meditating. I saw the wonders of meditation on Ming, the lady I befriended at the Mission. She meditated for thirty minutes every morning and evening for restorative sleep and remarkable tranquility.'

'Yes, I need to commit to that, Dr Deakin has advised consistency. I don't know if I can spare that time every day.'

'When it comes to your wellbeing, surely you can take an hour each day to save yourself, sister dear. Anyway, I'm ready to tell you about my adventures if you're up to listening to some of it, this morning.'

'I've invited Virginia over for dinner, and yes, I would love to hear more about your Mission adventure and perhaps you can call Felicity later while I'm preparing dinner. She won't forgive me if you don't call to tell her you're back!'

Grace, always in the role of big sister, reminded Patience of what she ought to be doing out of respect for those who loved her.

Patience started her story with what she firmly believed was staged turbulence, to divert the aircraft to its unnamed destination. She spoke of Akanya, the Indian national and her maternal manner, Audra the agitated American and Ming, the mindful, calm and humble, although fearful school teacher. She reiterated that they were not in any physical danger, the lack of contact with home was soul destroying.

'Thank you for setting up breakfast, outdoors. We were starved of natural light at the Mission. Locked away for three months felt like being in a bomb shelter, although every luxury was available. The artificiality of the place contrasted with the authenticity of the folk who inhabited the space. As much as having a bit of the outdoors in Pakistan, the Well Study Centre, where I spent most of the day, was underground.'

Grace listened without asking any questions, just absorbing everything, trying to understand what it was like for Patience under those conditions. She understood her sister would carry that need to be outdoors for a long time to come. Patience spoke of the enigmatic Masuyo and the hard life she had as a new mother in prison.

'She seems to be an amazing woman. I hope I get to meet her someday, to see her as you've described her.'

'Yeah, no ego, or self-righteous talk, but beneath the humility, a strength and commitment was fueled by her political ideology.'

'Who is responsible for the Mission, is it exclusively Masuyo's organisation?'

'I don't think so, she referred to instructions from HQ, but was mysterious about who headed the Mission. Nobody questioned her after her initial reluctance to share that information.'

'I can't believe you did not agitate to know more!'

'I assumed it was a government initiative affiliated to some global organisation. It is a massive operation, so the force behind it has tremendous power in the world, I daresay.'

'I saw the television interview when some passengers, or should I say recruits were released. One young, Swedish woman, I can't remember her name, said she was allowed to leave when she got ill. That gave me hope that you were not mistreated.'

'That would have been Alva. She was unhappy from the

outset when she realised we were not in Thailand, and had no access to the outdoors as such.'

'For one as young as her that would have been a stifling experience.'

'She is in her twenties like Zuri, Masuyo's daughter.'

When Patience provided every remembered detail on the Mission, Grace declared that it was a mystery that such an enormous organisation had successfully concealed its work from the world.

'It was very comfortable, I secretly called it *The Mother Ship*. Except for the tiniest shower, with my quarter pirouette moves, everything else was massive, fit for a queen.'

'It's beginning to make sense now, why you called it a life altering experience. It is almost as if you were on another planet, except for your shower, I suppose,' Grace smiled.

'It sure felt like that. I believe we were underground somewhere. The air conditioning ran twenty-four-seven to keep the place cool. It was a massive dome structure with no view of the sky and no windows looking out. That almost did my head in, I tell you. Awful! It seemed 'cultish' with the TUC greeting, that is 'Truth, Understanding, Compassion,' and kimonos and tracksuits with the TUC monogram, that we were required to wear – individuality had to be kept at bay. That unhinged poor Alva.'

'We need natural light, it keeps the mind alert, and the body healthy. I don't think I would have coped for as long as you did. I would have cracked like Alva and would have been sent home.'

They sat outside talking for two hours and had to stop as Virginia was coming over for dinner. They spent the afternoon in the kitchen, preparing roast lamb, gravy and grilled vegetables, chatting as they worked.

'Were there any clashes among the women, with being holed-up the way you all were.'

'I won't call it being 'holed-up' because the meeting venues were spacious. Akanya and Audra did come head-to-head once or twice but resolved their differences. TUC values ensured that Truth, Understanding and Compassion were followed.'

Grace slipped out, just before Virginia was due to arrive, to buy bread rolls and garlic bread while Patience called Felicity.

'It's wonderful to hear your voice, Patience. You had us in a frenzy when we lost contact with you. Are you well? Is there anything you need?' Felicity asked with gentle excitement.

'I am very well, thank you, the sound of your voice is all I need, right now. We have a lot of catching up to do. Thank you for all you've been doing to find us. Grace told me you went to The Hague and tried to shake up some action. I am also sorry that Alf's health is declining.'

'Well, going to The Hague was a fat waste of time – nothing really significant came from the waves I created! Yes, Alf is sinking, Patience.' Her voice cracked in trying to hide her emotions, something she always concealed. 'I would love to see you, girlfriend, I don't know when I can get away with things as they are.'

'We are planning a trip to Melbourne, soon.'

'That will be good, but forget your sister coming with that Irishman hanging onto her. Did you see the rock she's sporting, or hiding is more like it?'

'I sure did! She wants to come to Melbourne, and I look forward to the three of us being together again.'

'Really? I hope she does, we need some time together.'

After Patience provided a few sketchy details on her time away, Felicity voiced her views on Masuyo and the Mission.

'To me she is no enigma. She sounds like a needy woman who missed her calling somewhere along the line. As for that organisation, it is very unprofessional in putting the lives of its head-hunted recruits at risk.'

Patience preferred not to argue with Felicity. They parted with the promise to meet soon.

Grace met Virginia in the elevator, on her way up to the apartment, after her brief shopping spree for last minute forgotten dinner treats. After many years she saw a box of Beacon Superfine Chocolates in the confectionary aisle and could not resist picking up the last two boxes on the shelf. A taste of South Africa that she remembered with childhood fondness could not be ignored. Her father always bought a box for her mother's birthday, their wedding anniversary or on Valentine's Day. Today she was armed with the superfine memory of her parents.

Patience enjoyed the videos Virginia saved of Ajax and Sprite and their latest antics. She clapped her hands, laughed, did a little dance – the stillness in Grace's apartment was a thing of the past with her sister back.

'Thank you! You recorded every cute moment of my dog-babies. I really have to come home to see them!' She glanced over for Grace's reaction.

'We have twenty-four sister hours left yet, before you head off home!' Grace playfully cautioned. She needed far more than twenty-four Patience hours. So much remained unsaid. She had to summon the courage to speak out on her concerns regarding Keefe.

Virginia enjoyed their sisterly banter.

'You haven't changed, you look just as you did when you left. That tells me you were well cared for, right?' Virginia's overactive imagination had her believing that Patience was in a torture camp somewhere in the world and would never return.

'Yes, it gave the impression of being on a luxurious cruise ship on dry land! A fabulous place! The Mission folk were good people. It took me a while to figure that out, but they are great people working towards a better future.'

Virginia updated Patience on the latest at the Sisters Helping Sisters Organisation, and the new staff member, Lindiwe John-son. She had no intention of bogging Patience down with too many work details this soon. Much had changed during her absence with the growing demand for more safe houses.

'Sprite and Ajax might need a sedative when they see you,'

she joked. I have had a wonderful time with them, they are great companions. You've trained them well.'

'Stay on at the house as long as you want, don't feel pressured to leave with my return. It would be good to have adult, human company at home as I settle back into the groove of my civilian life!' She rolled her eyes and hugged Virginia. She was grateful that Grace identified the potential in Virginia after her ordeal at ER over a year ago. For the first time since she opened the SHSO, she had an assistant who made it possible for her to keep the organisation running with peace of mind during her trips away.

THE NEXT MORNING Patience set out for the SHSO office on a whim. Lindiwe Johnson greeted her at the entrance, unaware at first of who she was. She gasped when Patience introduced herself.

'Oh, my goodness, I'm so sorry, I didn't know you were coming in today. It's an absolute pleasure to meet you. I'm sure the media must be hot on your heels since your return, wanting the scoop on your story.'

'Far from it! Thankfully, it has been peaceful being back with my sister. Anyway, it's classified information, I don't have permission to share it with the media.'

Patience looked with curiosity at this newcomer in her organisation who appeared to be a tad overzealous about her return. Alarm bells sounded. How loyal is this woman to the organisation, can she be trusted? She fawns too much was her first impression.

Virginia called Lindiwe from the café downstairs to ask if she wanted coffee and was thrilled to learn that Patience was in the office. She came up with a box of crisp ham and cheese croissants, and coffee for a quick shared breakfast.

'You are just as bad as Grace. You both must stop feeding me. All I've been doing since my return is eat!'

'We're celebrating your return, and what better way than with decadent food! I'm taking you over to see Sprite and Ajax after coffee. They need to see you as much as you need to see them.'

Patience noted that Lindiwe watched them without smiling. She felt uneasy for the first time since her return.

'Let's go home! I can finish my coffee in the car. Nice to have met you, Lindiwe. See you again soon!' She rushed out the office, her second home for so many years – now she was uncomfortable there.

In the car she questioned Virginia.

'Are you happy with Lindiwe as the SHSO receptionist? She seems to be a nice woman.'

'We didn't have many applicants for the position, most were teenagers with no experience. Lindiwe was well-presented and had worked in social services before, that is why I chose her.'

'Fair enough, you had to choose the best applicant. I must admit I felt a little uneasy around her after she mentioned the media coming after my story. It's not my story to share, least of all with the media.'

'Don't worry, it's just her curiosity, she was shocked at what had happened to you. Most news broadcasts covered the story, soon after the flight disappeared. Grace kept away from media interference.'

'It could be me being sensitive, I guess. I have to get back to being 'normal' again.' She shrugged it off not to upset Virginia about her choice of staff.

AJAX AND SPRITE agitated to get out of the backyard when the car pulled up outside the house. Virginia let them out onto the front lawn. Memory flooded back for their beloved carer, mother, friend, and everything that Patience provided for them. They rivaled for her attention, wanting a pat on the head. The quiet suburban street erupted with peals of laughter and playful barks with Patience rolling on the lawn with her canine babies.

Virginia looked out the window and yelled out to her to come indoors. Too late! The television camera hovered above her face with the interviewer waving the microphone at her. They caught her in a most awkward, private moment.

'Ms Sharvin, where were you held captive? Were you subjected to physical abuse, where is the missing plane?'

Ajax and Sprite morphed from adoring babies into salivating, angry dogs. Low, menacing growls, and bared teeth had the reporters scurrying away. Patience rushed indoors and watched them walk away. The agitated crew demonstrated their frustration with their air punches and cussing as they headed to their vehicle – they would be back, it was the nature of the beast, chasing a story.

'That was a narrow escape. My boys saved the day! There's one thing I know for sure, my mothers were always right when they said, don't second guess instinct. Keep your guard up with Ms Lindiwe Johnson!'

3

MATTERS OF THE HEART

G race's irritation that the media had invaded Patience's life, so soon after her arrival, set her off on a tirade in her well-known disdain for the media and governments that assumed they were Big Brother.

Patience returned to Grace's apartment later that evening when the media set up camp across the street from her home, with a clear view of the comings and goings on her driveway.

'How utterly audacious to barge in on you like that!'

'It's pretty obvious they were tipped off.'

'Who? Virginia? It's not possible.'

'Never her! I believe it's the Johnson woman she employed as SHSO's receptionist!'

'You can't be serious, she seemed like a lovely person, when I met her.'

'My gut has never let me down, Grace.'

'Time to have a serious word with Virginia and perhaps Lindiwe Johnson.'

'I'll do that soon. Now, before there are any more distractions and because Keefe is coming over for breakfast tomorrow, I need to know what it is you're not telling me. If I am oblivious to what's happening, I might put my foot in it with Keefe, knowing my big mouth!'

Grace welled-up but was prepared to bring down the wall that separated her from her sister. She understood with past pain that keeping secrets was soul destroying. Patience would never judge her. They needed this quiet intimate time to reconnect with what they missed in each other's worlds. She struggled with how to begin.

'What is it Grace, what are you reluctant to tell me? I should be used to that, I know, but it's something you *have to* change.'

Grace sighed and looked away, 'I have been disappointed with Keefe of late.'

'You can't let things slide, you are obviously unhappy and need to speak up, not only to me, but to Keefe too.'

'How? Without sounding like an old coot? The thing is he's been drinking excessively lately. We rarely do things together these days. I miss him, Patience. He's slipping away, and I don't know what to do.'

Grace's pain was evident in her resigned tone, she was not one to admit she had failed or had no solutions to a problem. Things had got out of control between them.

'Speak to him in a sober state. Turn up at the hospital and have lunch with him. Could he be crumbling, possibly having a delayed grief reaction to his mother's death? Men are hopeless at talking about their vulnerabilities. It's up to you to get him to be frank about his problems.'

'He was very close to his mother, he briefly showed that sensitive side, now there's a barrier I can't get through.'

'Don't stress about this. Think through how you are going to broach his excessive drinking with him. He might appreciate that you are prepared to do this, to help him.'

'I'm thinking of ending the relationship. I don't want issues of this sort in my life. I've been alone this long, so I'm okay to go on that way.'

'Don't be rash, Grace. Wait until we can both figure the best course of action for you.' Patience feared that Grace would end what had the promise of the good life, she deserved.

'You don't need to add this burden to your life, you've come back home after a terrible ordeal and need to look after yourself. You need to move on with your life, Patience.'

'I've told you, it was only an ordeal until I could communicate with you. Please ensure you make the right decision in your relationship.' Patience convinced herself that her little family could survive anything.

'I'm so glad you're back. You are the only constant in my life, until you decide to go globetrotting again!'

'Not true, Andrew is a constant friend to you. Trust that relationship enough to sound out your concern with him about Keefe. A man's perspective is needed.'

'I suppose. What a waste I am, mending my patients and incapable of mending my own life.'

'You are the best medic I know, so let us remember that.'

'I wish I could believe that these days. We lost a baby in ER not so long ago. A beautiful baby girl to lovely parents. They were devastated.'

'You should take Keefe's advice on letting it go, to save yourself. Now let's decide when you are going to talk to him about how you are feeling about his erratic behaviour.' Patience pulled Grace back, she was not going to be side-tracked by ER stories when her sister's life was in a mess.

'I don't know if I want to do that. He's an adult and we are in a new relationship. This tells me he doesn't care about my feelings.'

'Ridiculous! He is hopelessly in love with you. He is under some stress that needs attention. I will observe him tomorrow and let you know my thoughts. Then, you should act on how to proceed. Leaving things as it is, is not what Mama Varuna would want for you.'

Grace listened with arrested attention to what Patience

offered as a solution. She accepted that she had to speak to Keefe if she hoped to turn the situation around. Her anxiety surfaced in anticipation of Patience's reactions when Keefe came over in the morning.

KEEFE ARRIVED the next day laden with pastries and the aroma of deep-roasted coffee for three. He gave Grace a peck on the cheek, put down his bag of breakfast delights and reached out to bear-hug Patience. His joy in seeing her with Grace was obvious.

'Wonderful to see you looking so well, Patience!'

'Thank you, Keefe, it's good to be home.'

Grace's rosy-pink cheeks and edginess spelt her unease in Keefe's company. She hoped that it would not make her sister uncomfortable to see them distant with each other. Patience saw their crumbling relationship, in that moment. Keefe avoided eye-contact with Grace. His former loving disposition was aloof, yet not cold. They both had faced some hurt that they had buried deep inside. She felt compelled to lift this impasse between them.

'I was supposed to have breakfast ready for you, not you, bringing us breakfast with these fattening pastries.' Grace growled in an uncharacteristic tone.

Patience jumped in to save them both any further embarrassment.

'I love pastries for brekky, as you know, sis. Thanks, Keefe.' She smiled with a stern look at Grace to curb her tongue.

'I didn't want you working in the kitchen while I chatted with Patience, so I decided to do this. Come, mo ghrá, don't be upset, you can prepare a meal for us all, another day.' He was desperate to keep things amicable between them with Patience around.

Keefe looked thinner too, not as she remembered. His face was gaunt, his cheeks flattened. He wore a pair of jeans and an oversized jumper. The skinny-leg jeans showed off his pale ankles, and obvious sockless feet in a pair of brown suede loafers.

'You look relaxed this morning, Keefe,' she lied, 'how has work been these days? Have you settled in well to life as an Aussie medic?'

'Aye, I sure have. I have also been going to bed earlier since you arrived. I've been forbidden to stop by around here while you are staying over,' he laughed, then looked at Grace with a mixture of hurt and guilt. Troubled couples could not keep up appearances for long, the cracks were widening, and Patience felt helpless with no context other than Grace's complaint on Keefe's excessive drinking.

'Thank you for respecting our need for sisterly time.' She was gracious to add while Grace remained silent, busying herself with slicing cheese and ham to complement their pastry breakfast.

A cool breeze wafted in through the balcony door. Grace excused herself to fetch a cardigan from the bedroom.

'You are alive to tell the tale, Patience. I tell you what, there were many speculations about your whereabouts. Tell me about this Mission you were on. Grace was in quite a tizzy when news broke that the plane had disappeared.'

'Yeah, poor Grace, I would have had the same reaction in her position.'

'Aye, I know what you mean. I'm very close to my sister, Aileen too.'

'Oh, pardon me for rudely not acknowledging the passing of your mother.' Patience jumped up and hugged Keefe, 'I'm so sorry, Keefe.'

A veil shadowed his usually radiant blue eyes. He looked out the balcony door for a few quiet seconds, then responded.

'Aye, mam struggled in the last weeks of her life. She is at peace now.'

Patience reached across and squeezed his hand. Compassion was her natural reaction when she saw pain in those around her.

'Thank you, Patience. Now tell me some interesting details about your trip. This is a joyous time, having you safely back home. Let's not mar it with talk of sadness.'

All Patience saw in this man, was a caring soul. Perhaps he veered off into his own sadness. Grace had to have a face-to-face chat with him to understand the cause of their issues. She returned with a red cardigan, still silent and withdrawn.

'You look gorgeous in red, mo ghrá!'

Grace ignored Keefe's compliment.

'Have your coffee before it gets too cold, we can chat at the table.'

'Aye, you are right mo ghrá. We can always trust you to get us back on task.' Grace turned a deeper shade of pink, and Patience wondered whether his comment might have been sarcastic.

She hoped to ease their tension by speaking of her days at the Mission and the people she met. She mentioned her suspicion when she heard the departing helicopter late one night, followed by news of Alva being sent home for her poor health.

Grace piped in on that point, repeating what she had already told Patience to avoid any direct conversation with Keefe.

'Yes, that Current Affairs piece on the women who left the Mission because of ill health, gave us hope that this might not be a terrorist organisation after all.'

Keefe applauded Andrew for alerting them to the television interview that calmed Grace about her sister's safety.

'I believed that you might have been at some remote location, if the women had to be airlifted, perhaps there was no vehicle access to where you were. These thoughts crossed my mind.'

'To this day, I have no idea where we were. Amazing, is the only way I can define the experience. It's baffling how this was concealed from so many of us. I had a nagging thought that I could have been in Australia when I had to board the flight for Karachi from Perth. I'm still not sure about that either.'

Grace slipped into the conversation although limiting direct interactions with Keefe – hostility continued to brew beneath the surface for her. Patience insisted that she would tidy up after breakfast to allow them time together.

She overheard Keefe, 'When can I come over to spend the night, mo ghrá? I miss being around you these days.'

Grace whispered, 'Not now. We need to talk through a few matters before we decide on that.'

Patience felt the sting for Keefe. The relationship signaled that it was close to being over.

After Keefe left around midday, she toyed with the idea of chatting to Grace about her observations.

'I hope things were not too awkward for you with Keefe coming over.' Thankfully Grace opened the conversation.

'Not at all, he's the same lovely person I met before I left for South Africa. I don't quite understand what the problem is between you. He too, looks rather skinny these days. You both are stubborn and need to have an honest conversation with each other.'

'Oh, please stop with the weight thing! It's not easy to talk to a man who clearly thinks nothing is wrong. You heard him, he wants to spend more nights here.'

The minute she uttered her irritation, she regretted it.

'I'm sorry, I don't mean to be unkind. You are concerned because you love us, and here I go snapping at you. I'm really sorry sis.'

'No need to apologise. Just have the big conversation with him sooner rather than later.'

'I will, I told him we need to talk. Hopefully he realises that things are off colour between us. Men can be blind to these matters.'

'Avoid the negativity and save the relationship. It's worth saving, unless it's Andrew you want to encourage!'

'No, I don't want to encourage him, it took long enough for him to realise that I had no romantic inclination towards him!'

Patience lightened the moment for Grace with her little sister advice and fun.

'Call him now and set up a date and then I'll tell you about Judd Knight.' Patience was relentless that Grace had to act – love lost was more painful than love never found.

'Not now, who is Judd Knight? I thought you were on a women's only program. I'm intrigued.'

Patience had Grace laughing at Masuyo's reaction when she told her she had a human need for male company and described how the ladies responded to the charming Judd.

She was taken by surprise when Grace asked her, 'So when are you going to meet the man, or woman of your dreams? You have a lot of advice to offer in that department.'

4

TRUTH

Patience arrived at the SHSO offices in a huff.

A face-to-face discussion with Lindiwe on her involvement on the media intrusion at her home had to be thrashed out.

Grace was an intensely private person, Patience was the social butterfly in the family, yet both abhorred unwelcome attention in their lives. The passive and outgoing pair were fierce in their pursuit of privacy. Instinct told Patience that Lindiwe had a part to play in her stolen precious time with Sprite and Ajax.

She called Virginia from the street downstairs.

'Hey, Virginia, sorry to disturb you this early in the day. Can you slip out of the office for five minutes, to meet me downstairs? Please don't let Lindiwe know you're meeting me.'

'Sure, I'll be down now, I hope everything is okay, Patience.'

'All will make sense, soon. Please hurry.'

Patience's diplomacy was primed, she had to have her suspicions confirmed.

'I apologise for my unceremonious visit today, but I have to act in the heat on this before another media fiasco.'

'Has something more happened after that horrible incident?'

'Thankfully, no, but Grace saw a media vehicle outside her apartment block and believes they might know I was staying at her place. Perhaps it's a coincidence, but I have this doubt, which I need to sound out with Lindiwe. Are you with me on this?'

'Absolutely! Do you think she has something to do with it? I feel awful for hiring her, if she is guilty of doing this.'

'A strong hunch makes me think she is involved in some way. How would you know anything apart from the credentials on her resume and interview she presented? Don't worry yourself over that.'

Lindiwe gave them a cheery greeting as they entered the office foyer. Her charm, mellow voice and flirtatious tone was her appealing trait. She was a good reception desk person for any business.

'What a lovely surprise, Patience! I was not expecting you back at work, so soon.'

'Hi Lindiwe, no, not back officially yet. I have a few things to attend to. I am still reeling from the media invasion at my home. Do you perhaps know anything on how that came to pass?' Patience's direct manner, her unmistakable strength that saved many deceptive situations from getting out of hand, was bristling. Masuyo admired that quality in her, seeing her as trustworthy, and deserving of her respect.

Lindiwe's awkward silence, at first, convinced Patience that her suspicions were correct. What she needed to know was the extent of her involvement and whether she had an agenda in applying for the position at the SHSO.

'I... er... am not sure why you ask, but you should be pleased that this will give the SHSO and you, some exposure, fame you know.' She batted her thick mascaraed eyelids at Patience.

'This is not some celebrity organisation. We run safe houses for women in violent relationships. How did you not understand our mission statement in applying for your position? Privacy is vital for the safety of our women.'

Virginia cowered behind Patience. Never had she seen Patience livid, and unafraid to make it known.

'Oh, no... sorry, I did not mean for it to come across that way... it's just... er... well...'

'Please say what's on your mind, just speak plainly, that's all I ask.'

'Am I fired?' Lindiwe whispered.

'I don't remember saying that!' Answer my question. What do you know about the media coming over to my home? It's a simple question. You either know something, or you know nothing at all. Which is it, Lindiwe?

Patience was strong, but she detested confrontations. At any cost she would uphold the SHSO ethos and beware the person who tried to muddy the organisation's reputation in the community! Fame and fortune were not her goals, her selfless, caring and ever ready nature in saving a distressed person, was her priority. She waited for Lindiwe's response.

'The media called twice in the week you arrived from your overseas assignment. First, the local newspaper called, and then the television news channel.'

'I suspected they had a heads-up on my return to Australia. What did they want? More importantly, what did you say?'

Lindiwe pinched the loose skin on her left hand, nervous about where to begin, and how to convince Patience that she was not responsible for what happened.

'I'll admit, I told them you might be coming to the office sometime this week, but that they should speak to you directly.'

'Why were you silent about this when I came to the office that day? You did not think it important to mention to Virginia, your manager, that they were sniffing around?'

'I did not think they would turn up at your home. I have nothing to do with that, please believe me.' Lindiwe's stress in her high-pitched tone, signaled that she feared that her job was in jeopardy for something she did not intend to happen.

For a tightrope-tense minute, Patience stared at Lindiwe trying to figure out what to believe from the charming Ms Johnson. Loyalty meant everything to her. Mama Varuna insisted that she and Grace uphold trust and loyalty as sisters, in their childhood and as adults, if they hoped to sustain their relationship, in the true sense of *for life*. The reason she offered for this insistence was that apartheid South Africa divided people and some chose misplaced trust over truth. Foregoing loyalty was selling one's soul to the devil, she stressed. People who became soulless under that unjust regime, were soon driving expensive cars and going on extravagant overseas holidays without legitimate earnings nor tax obligations to match.

'Your negligence in all of this is firstly in not alerting Virginia to those calls from the media. I believe by you giving them the information on when I was coming to the office, led to them waiting outside, to follow Virginia and I to my home.'

Lindiwe's insistence on her lack of involvement, was silenced. She shuffled her feet, looked away, and said in an inaudible voice, 'I'm so sorry, I did not realise they would do something like that... until you said...'

'This won't be the end of it, for sure. They want a story and will make up one if they must. They know where I live now and perhaps where my sister lives. Virginia and I have to be super-alert for their prowling around the house.'

Virginia piped in for the first time, 'Yes, this means we might have to hire a security guard at the house, and one to watch you, Patience.'

'I'm so sorry for all this trouble to you both.'

Patience's annoyance had escalated to a point of no return in being gentle with Lindiwe that morning.

'Too late for tears, I'm afraid. The damage has been done. I worry about you being alone, Virginia. I have to stay away from the house for a while longer.'

'Should I pack my stuff and leave, have I been fired?'

'Don't let me repeat myself. You are NOT fired but have to undergo some training on the protocol around here on matters of privacy.'

Patience and Virginia went into a meeting to discuss matters. They left a relieved Lindiwe to mull over her stupidity. She raised her palms in salutation as she walked out of Patience's office. All that mattered to her was that her job was safe.

'Nobody exasperates me as much as she does. She presses all the wrong buttons!'

'I'm truly sorry for employing her.' Virginia groaned, close to tears. 'I think we should ask her to leave immediately.'

Patience knew the logical thing was to dismiss Lindiwe, but foresight kicked in.

'I don't think that would be wise. We do not want an angry employee out there, mouthing off to the media. They are hungry for a story – it's the ratings that count for them.'

Virginia in all her naiveté of the business world, was skeptical in accepting that idea, and in need of a basic Business 101 lesson from Patience.

'Do you believe this will be possible?'

'People do strange things at the best of times, Lindiwe is a classic example. She dropped a careless word with no thought for the repercussions. That surprises me because she is a mature woman with life experience. Yet I am inclined to think she basks in receiving attention, albeit negative, and will do anything to get it.'

Patience acknowledged that Lindiwe erred in being human. Lord knows, her friend, and associate, Felicity Cassano, was guilty of many a faux pas in their time together.

'What do you propose we do with her?'

'I don't intend getting rid of her, if we have a life lesson to give her. She will grow from it once she understands our values here at the SHSO!'

'You amaze me, every time. Will you send her for training?'

'I will be doing the training. She will be 'Patiencenised,' as it were!' Laughter eased Virginia's self-inflicted guilt for inviting Lindiwe into the organisation. Letting go, was something Patience believed served her well through her own life traumas. Virginia was astounded by Patience's sense of *a fair go,* she lived it in all that she did.

GRACE ADMITTED that seeing Keefe face-to-face that morning was good to air what she thought had gone wrong in their relationship. He accepted that he had been drinking far more than he could hold down, and that he struggled with insomnia in recent weeks, hence his general lack-lustre attitude towards her. He guarded against revealing what truly bothered him. He was open to the idea of seeing Dr Deakin to help him cope with his drinking and whatever else lay hidden in the crevices of his mind.

Patience listened with no interruptions until Grace finished saying what she had to say.

'Twin souls! That's what you both are! You both bottle things up until it explodes! The warning signs splutter away and you both pretend everything is just hunky-dory!' Patience pulled a face and laughed. Laughter for the second time that day provided needed release from tension. She was happy that her sister had chosen the proactive path, this time. It could only get better with this approach.

'What's the situation with Lindiwe Johnson? Are you letting her go?' Grace asked with trepidation, aware that Patience, too, had had a strenuous people morning.

'On the contrary, she will stay and learn the SHSO way. If I fail, then she will get her marching orders.'

'You are your name, that's been proven many times over. If it was me, on the other hand, I would have put in a demand for the order of the boot!'

'Yes, Mama Elsie's wise burden that she left me with, a namesake I have to honour. Bless her.' Patience glowed with the memory of her gentle, silent mother.

'I might be Grace, but in name only, I don't have your equanimity.'

'You don't see what I see in you, you have been patient with Keefe, and in waiting for my return. You are gracious in so many ways. On equanimity, you should have seen me this morning. I had Virginia shivering in fear, unsure of when to speak.' Patience clapped her hands and laughed again. Every opportunity that presented itself drew her towards the humour in things. It was her survival mechanism. Grace considered whether her sister's humour stemmed from culture or perhaps it was innate to her personality.

'Life lessons come from love, anger, joy and so much more, I suppose.'

'Can we *not* talk about the Mission tonight? I would like to hang out with my sister, drinking some gin, watching a soppy movie, and just be girls, please.'

'Oh dear, I think I might have ruined such an evening for us.'

'Why, what have you done? Hired some male strippers? O-la-la! Okay, sorry that's a bit far-fetched. Pray do tell before I burst!'

'Andrew asked if he could come over to see you. I agreed that we would have drinks with him. I could reschedule, he's easy going.'

'No, please don't cancel. It might be good to have company.'

'He is as thoughtful as Keefe in wanting to bring us dinner. I protested, but knowing him, he will bring your fav Thai dishes.'

Patience was stoked to hear Grace's first positive comment on Keefe, since her return, and a Thai dinner might be just what she needed after her dreadful morning.

'You love Keefe, sis. That Freudian slip was a dead giveaway!' Another outburst of cackling laughter had Grace throwing a cushion at Patience.

'Stop that! Now you'll have me watching everything I say

around you. On a serious note, bless the day you returned! I am putting a strap around your ankles and tying you to the couch! You are not leaving anytime soon anywhere, if I have anything to do with it!'

'When big sister speaks, I obey!' Patience bowed in mocked respect.

Little did she know that the longevity of her response was not a certainty.

5

MEMORIES

Patience found emotional comfort in Grace's apartment and her old bed. The reconnection to place is vital to every traveler who returns after a long spell of absence.

She lay in bed that morning listening to the sounds of waking birds, undeterred by the bustling sounds of traffic and other human cacophony in this vast metropolis. People hurried into their working day afraid to be late for the train, bus, ferry, early morning meeting... hurrying into a world that threatened not to wait, chasing the clock every day. In this worried rush nobody stopped to see the sun appear over rooftops. Unnoticed beauty lost in the need to be everywhere, in every waking moment.

Grace was accustomed to the jarring early morning sounds, something that allowed her a sense of safety. She enjoyed her solitude but needed the thought that human help was not too far off. As much as she vehemently proclaimed to be over her attack in her early days, as an intern, in South Africa, she barricaded herself in at night. Triple locks and dead locks secured her front door and balcony sliding door. Fear lurked in the hinterland of memory. Patience, on the other hand, loved wide open spaces, unaffected by the need for constant home security, even though she was held up, in her home, by an irate husband whose wife had been placed at the SHSO safe house in Sydney.

Two sisters, yin and yang, or gin and tonic, similar and yet so different. Sisters from different mothers who spent their child-hood as one family. The melodious sounds of birds, celebrating a new dawn, melted thoughts of the concrete jungle around her. She missed the naturalness of the sun, sky, grass and melodic birdsongs when she was locked away in a place that was never named. She loved her home, set in an uncluttered street with a sprawling, lush, front lawn and wide backyard.

She mulled over how much she had taken for granted, she inhaled in gratitude for the Sydney home she could return to.

They had a cosy evening with Andrew Lang with neither of them concerned about fussing over what to wear, or whether more mascara was essential. He visited to see Grace's happiness with her sister being home. No doubt, Grace was in an enviable position with a young man basking in her company, one who accepted being spurned in love because their friendship mattered more. His connection to Grace was his lifeline, she made feel him feel like family. Now he was as much Grace's younger brother as he was hers. Close friendships were vital to them when family turned their back on her widowed mother. Cruel, callous family readily condemned – too free and easy they said. Felicity was an unstinting loyal friend, and Virginia a godsend in wanting to assist with the SHSO, during her months at the Mission. Ming too had become a dear friend.

Patience flicked through photographs on her phone. Akanya's round-faced smile, and open lotus palm with her other arm tucked around Patience's shoulder reflected her free, open and often fun-loving nature. Something innately spiritual in Ming's quiet smile and inclining head, added to her appealing humility. No photographs of the others at the Mission existed. Masuyo, Zuri, Xandria and Alexis were ghost-memories of those days. Not a single photograph of the surroundings of their unnamed location existed. She wondered how she coped for all those months with no access to her mobile phone. That indicated that dependence was a state of mind.

The aroma of percolating coffee interrupted her reverie when Grace called out.

'I know you're awake, Patience! Come grab a cuppa while it's steaming hot.'

She was due on shift later that evening and wanted to get in a few more Patience hours before she had her afternoon nap. ER nights were increasingly busy in the last three weeks. She needed to be energised and alert for whatever walked through the doors that night.

Her hair tied up in a ponytail gave her a youthful appearance.

'Morning, you! Still enjoying your old bed, I see.'

'It sure is good. Mmmmm... this coffee is amazing, what is it? I can't pick it.'

Grace picked up a bag of coffee beans from the kitchen counter, holding the bag up, she inhaled deeply.

'This is it. Andrew got me a few bags from a coffee expo he attended.'

'Oh, that Andrew, rather, YOUR Andrew, he is a doting puppy, always bringing treats for Ms Gracie!' she laughed, 'he knows you well, this *is* superb coffee.'

She allowed Patience to get away with this taunt.

They chatted over coffee on her days at the Mission, the gracious way Masuyo allowed a cultural cooking session day to bring the women closer in appreciation of their difference, and the joy of togetherness in a shared meal. Grace suggested that Masuyo must have had extensive leadership training in knowing how to manage people in harmonising common goals.

'Yes, she was a strategist. She appealed to people to win more support and used women and food as an inroad to achieve her goals. I think she missed her calling as a psychologist!'

Patience continued that Masuyo was difficult to understand at the beginning because of her changeable nature, but soon she discovered that their leader was no different from the rest.

Grace interrupted Patience in the middle of her recollections.

'I think your phone is ringing in the bedroom.'

Her sense of hearing was deliberately fine-tuned. She ensured she prepared for whatever followed the sounds in her life. The perpetual strains of Boetie Arendse's song, prior to his attack, made her a *sound detective* of everything she heard in her daily life.

Patience was annoyed that she had missed the call from Ming.

'It must be pretty early in the morning there. I'll call her as soon as we finish our coffee. No big breakfast, please, sis. Bran is all I can tolerate this morning. You have been feeding me like I'm the one needing to be fattened!' She clapped her hands and laughed her husky, joyous laugh.

'I have some paperwork to update and need a nap for an hour before my shift, if I'm to survive the night.'

'I'll call Ming.'

AT 10 AM Patience called China.

'Ming Xu! How are you girlfriend?' Patience chuckled. 'I was looking through the photographs Zuri took of us just before we left the Mission. I willed you to call!'

After a momentary pause, a familiar gentle voice answered.

'I am very well, thank you, Patience. It's good to speak to you again. You must be enjoying the time with your dear sister.'

'It's so good to hear you too, and yes Grace and I are in our second childhood, not in old age, but little girls again. I'm still staying over at her place.'

'How wonderful! I got straight back to work, and I am enjoying being back with my students.'

'Great! To what do I owe the pleasure of your earlier surprise call, apart from the fact that you love me, and miss me?'

A sigh elicited by the tension that she was the bearer of bad news made Ming drop any further social small talk.

'I don't suppose you've had news from Masuyo. I had a disturbing message from Zuri saying that Akanya is reported missing in India. Her staff at the technology school say they last saw her two days ago.'

'Missing? Could she not have gone off to see someone, or took a holiday?'

'I don't have any details so that's the baffling thing. What should we do?'

Just as she did at the Mission, Ming always sought out Patience's thoughts on matters that disturbed her.

'Ask Zuri for more information. I could call Akanya's staff there, a Goanese lady, Ojala, that she spoke of, to get more information.'

'That's a great idea, thank you, Patience.'

'Not to worry. Tell me the best time to call you, if I have any information on the situation.'

'I will be teaching, a text message alert will be good, to allow me to get someone to mind my students while I take your call.'

They parted, unsettled with the news. It was not possible that Akanya left on a whim. She expressed wanting to be back home during the early days at the training camp, and Masuyo did not take too kindly to her asking if she could call her colleagues when they were sent out on the field to different locations after their training.

Grace returned to the lounge and caught Patience's worried, perplexed look.

'You're lost in thought, there. Is everything okay, with Ming?

'I'm not sure what to think. I must call India in a few hours to find out what's happened to Akanya Das. She has apparently been missing for two days now. I pray she is unharmed, wherever she is. You should rest. Don't let this trouble you.'

OjALA DIYA at the Panna Centre was surprised and nervous when Patience called her. Akanya shared Ojala's contact details because she had family in Australia and had planned to visit them when Akanya returned to India.

When she realised, Patience was privy to intimate details of Akanya's childhood trauma, she relaxed in sharing what she knew.

Akanya's half-brother, Biddhu resurfaced, two decades later, after being adopted as a toddler. He was born after her widowed mother became a victim to unsavoury men in the district who took advantage of her situation.

She left to meet Biddhu in Delhi, and never returned. She wanted him to move closer to Panna with his family to allow her to see them often. He made a trip to Panna to reconnect with her. Ojala recalled her happiness in being reunited with family at this stage of her life. She sent him off with money, clothes for his children, and the promise of a visit to Delhi, to meet her family.

The police had done nothing to step up a search for Akanya, offering a disinterested attitude saying, 'all these women run off, thinking the grass is greener on the other side. Soon she will come back, you just have to wait until she decides to return.' No amount of convincing them that Akanya had not 'run off' received acknowledgement. With no contact details to reach Biddhu, Patience was at a loss on how to proceed in offering Ojala assistance. She promised to investigate what she could from Australia – she felt awful about her hollow promise. She feared that Akanya might have been injured and perhaps lying comatose in a hospital somewhere in India. It would be impossible to find her. Time and many people were needed to sift through the whereabouts of millions of missing women.

Locating Biddhu might be the best option. She would have to turn to the Mission for assistance. This had to be done through Zuri who was in contact with Ming.

Grace returned to the lounge two hours later, Patience was leaning over the balcony, still pensive, unaware of the trickling rain. Their light-hearted coffee morning took a turn they had not expected. Patience was sombre, unable to focus with anxious visions on Akanya's situation. Her jovial spirit dried up. Grace left for her ER shift, and Patience called Virginia to say she would work from home.

'I am really sorry for this last-minute change. A close friend is in trouble in India, and I need some time to check out a few things.'

'No need to apologise, let me know when you want to tap into the data here, I'll give you the passcode for remote access.'

'Great. You really have jacked-up the system. It was an office for one for so many years. Thanks for understanding.'

'Yeah, there were times, while you were away when I needed to update files in the evening or over weekends so remote access was an easy option without having to go in the next day and copy and paste information. SHSO is growing as we speak. We had fifteen new women in the Melbourne safe house this week, alone. Easy access to everything is vital.'

'I am so grateful to have you assisting me.'

Patience searched for information on Biddhu Das, unsure if he shared the same surname with Akanya, given the nature of his birth, and their mother's mental state.

Ojala said that Akanya's packed bag was left on her bed – something she would not have left behind if she planned to go to Delhi for a few days. Could Akanya have been side-tracked by someone or something and might perhaps still be in Panna? Thoughts wafted in and out on her perceptions of Akanya as a special 'chosen one' at the Mission. Audra believed that Akanya had privilege over the others. What was her hidden association with the organisation? Her thoughts were interrupted by several pings from her mobile phone.

Ming requested whether Masuyo could liaise directly with her. In the middle of replying, a message from Ojala popped up.

The words sent her heart into a palpitation overdrive.

Tourists were exploring the area near the Ken River and found a body on the river bank. It has allegedly been identified that it's Biddhu.

That stopped her internet search. She looked up the location of the Ken River, over an hour's drive from where Akanya lived. By foot it would have to be a nine-hour trek. Could she have been driven there, or did she go there at all? These questions sent a shiver down her spine.

If there's one thing she knew about Akanya, it was that she was a survivor.

She was determined to find the answers to her whereabouts.

6

FELICITY TO THE RESCUE

F elicity was pleased that Patience was finally making that trip to Melbourne. She was keen to know more on Akanya's situation.

Grace canceled going with Patience at the last minute, Andrew Lang had had an emergency appendectomy, there was no cover for her weekend shift, and he needed her assistance. She was the only friend he had in Sydney.

Felicity insisted, like only Felicity could, that Patience spend the weekend at her home. She accepted with reluctance, not wanting to disturb the high-care health routine Alf was undergoing. He asked for palliative care to be set up in his home. A full-time resident nurse attended to his medical needs.

'I should have booked in at the bed and breakfast place, it's just five minutes away. Nothing should come in the way of Alf's treatment sessions, I might be a hinderance.'

'Nonsense! Alf asked for you to stay here. I think he will enjoy hearing our laughter, it will be good for him.'

Patience could not imagine how she would be laughing while watching Alf fade away. Felicity could be insensitive at the worst of times.

'As long as you promise, not to wait on me. I don't want you to neglect Alf while I'm here.'

'Neglect Alf? That's ludicrous! He has a nurse beside him twenty-four-seven, and I am here. Now, stop quibbling about what's been settled. Tell me about your Mission experience. I need to know the minute details.'

In Felicity's territory Patience understood she would have to do as she was told. She spoke of her time there as an 'experience' not a 'training program.' Felicity congratulated Patience for looking well after the difficulties she faced. Their long-standing friendship allowed them to accept each other's foibles. Grace remained on the fringes of their association with Felicity. The conversation drifted to Akanya's unexplained disappearance.

'Trying to find her will not be easy, you know. It seems that nobody is quite clear where she was the day she went missing.'

Felicity's frown lines had deepened in recent weeks. She lived with the constant stress of Alf's declining health. He was several years her senior which came with the understanding that on life's journey, he could make his exit at any time. Longevity was not theirs to share. Felicity's forthright question, unlike Grace who was often indirect or avoided matters that distressed her, left Patience unsure of how to respond.

'Will you be going to India, then?'

After a brief pause, she replied, 'I have not given that a thought, but it is a possibility now that I think about it.'

'Don't you dare! You just got back. Grace will have another breakdown if you do!'

Her three frown lines creased and released, revealing dregs of foundation caked in the grooves. She was always meticulous and fashionable. Today she wore crumpled jeans, an oversized cotton shirt, and a pair of black beach tongs that exposed her chipped nail varnish. Her fortnightly trips to the nail salon was her ritual. It was clear that all her time went to caring for Alf, yet she would not acknowledge that. She was not sentimental on any matter apart from her passion on women's issues.

'I think you shouldn't rush over to India, too soon. Wait for more information, first. I could tap into a few contacts there. Also, the imbalance of gender power will be like penetrating a fortress.'

'You have too much going on now. I will keep in touch with Ming, for updates.'

'I know a supreme court judge in India, one of very few women in this role. We met at a legal conference in Hyderabad. I will get in touch with her. She's retired but will have influence in that department. Trying from our end, is better than waiting, as everyday lost complicates the matter. The agency there does not appear to be doing anything, from what you say.'

'Yes, this is true. Akanya's assistant, Ojala, believes nothing is being done to find her. Thank you, Felicity, for always coming to rescue the problems I can't solve.'

No matter where in the world, a woman needed assistance, and if it was within her power, Felicity would devote her time and energy to assist. Both were committed to women's issues, often putting themselves last. Felicity was raised in many abusive foster homes, she appreciated that one helping hand was sometimes all that was needed to ease pain and suffering. Grace remained a silent partner in their endeavours, given her reclusive nature, but she too was passionate on women's issues. All three in their angst and joy improved the lives of a multitude of women who came to them for assistance.

That night Patience had a whispered conversation with Grace in trying not to disturb Alf's routine in the next room.

'How are things with Alf? Poor Felicity, she must be so anxious.'

At times like this, Grace pulled in her medic head, and spoke from the heart.

'She's well, Grace. It's poor Alf that I'm concerned for. He insisted on high care at home. The room is set up like an ICU facility, but I worry that not everything is on hand should an emergency arise. Felicity knows best, I suppose. She's honouring his wish. That says a lot about how much she loves him.'

'Gosh, it's admirable that she lives her vows to the fullest, sadly not many do in this situation. Has she taken a long-service break from work?'

'She works from home these days and has video conferences with staff. She's aged since I last saw her, under the stress with all she's doing, but won't admit she's stretched.'

Patience appreciated that Grace was noble in her acknowledgement of the sacrifice Felicity made in caring for Alf. She was the recipient of many unfair criticisms from Felicity over the years on her passive nature and anxieties. She expected Grace to be as strong as she was.

'What's the buzz with Keefe now? Any plans?'

'We are spending the day together tomorrow. He had his first session with Dr Deakin. I hope he wants to debrief after his session, to let me in on what troubles him.'

Patience couched her next question with care. Grace was in a vulnerable state, although she denied it, saying she had control of the situation.

'Would you both consider a counseling session together?'

'Why? He might want privacy and lord knows I understand that.'

'Just as support... you could ask him...'

'He has to deal with whatever it is first. I will gladly step in should the need present itself.'

Patience stopped when she heard her sister's underlying irritation.

'That's a practical solution, I'm letting my emotions cloud my thinking here.' Patience giggled like she always did in awkward situations. There was no point in adding to Grace's problems.

A restless night followed her conversation with Grace. Life threw them situations when they least expected it. Akanya's disappearance, Alf's deteriorating health, and Keefe's emotional baggage was too much going on all at once between them. In all this Grace waged a silent war of the heart. Nothing was within their grasp – what change may come with things as they were, meant they had to adapt to survive.

The next morning Felicity insisted they go out to breakfast. Alf requested that she get out and about with Patience. He was happy with her choice of nurse and wanted her to have a relaxing morning with the only woman whose company elicited the best in her.

Patience popped her head in to check on Alf. He reached out to touch her hand, she pressed his hand gently and whispered, 'You going to be okay while Felicity is out?'

His frail voice was heartbreaking, 'Felicity needs you. Go, talk to her, make her happy.'

'Thank you, Alf, only if you're sure about this.'

She swallowed hard to hold back her tears, when he nodded and smiled. There was something to be said about the love of an older man in his concern for his partner's need for private time and space. This selfless love is what she hoped Grace would have. In her own life, she consciously accepted that she would never find such love. The women who came to her SHSO was all she needed at this point in her life. It was her choice to remain romantically unattached.

1932 Café and Restaurant on Collins Street was their favourite haunt when Patience was in Melbourne. She loved the ambiance of the décor and enjoyed being transported to an earlier period. Her visits to the museum, and art gallery, losing herself in history and culture provided the escape she needed from the SHSO – the hardship the women suffered, and who could forget, the annoying Lindiwe! In recent years, work pressure did not allow time for the respite she craved. The bond between Sydney and Melbourne was as much about place as it was about people. She recalled their mother being disappointed that Grace had a job offer in Country New South Wales. Varuna loved Melbourne, but soon she was a Sydney-sider who proudly proclaimed the title. They gained strength from her, and imbibed tranquility from Elsie. Two loving, supportive mothers steered their life decisions. It was no surprise when Grace chose to be a medic, and Patience a social worker.

Patience's favourite meal of the day had her deliberating over the menu. A turmeric latte, and a Manchester breakfast was enough protein to keep her satiated for the rest of the day. Felicity kept it light, not having much of an appetite these days.

'Is that all you're having? Eggs on toast? I feel guilty with my loaded plate.'

'You go for it, you enjoy the food here, and don't visit often enough. My appetite has waned with exhaustion and stress.' Patience heard Felicity's struggle in those words.

'I understand, so I won't bully you into eating more. I'll just eat it all!' she laughed for the first time since her arrival in Melbourne.

'And how I've missed your mirth. I am so glad we got out this morning. You were pent-up at the house, Alf wants things to be as normal as possible around him. Please relax and let him hear your laughter that he so enjoys.'

'I'll try.'

'Will you help me plan his funeral?'

Patience looked away, awkward and shocked at the request when Alf was still breathing.

'I'm sorry, does it make you uncomfortable talking about funerals?'

'No, it's not in my cultural head to plan a funeral in the living days. We take a week after death, or more to arrange it...'

Felicity had never seen Patience lower her head and avoid eye contact before.

'I think because your father and Graces' father were

murdered, and Varuna died in a car crash, is perhaps still a sore point for you.'

Patience wanted Felicity to stop! She rambled on about death in a matter-of-fact way. Her noted bluntness left Patience queasy this time. Her parents' deaths were not what she wanted to talk about that morning.

'Yeah, that's what it is. Culturally, we do not prepare for a funeral when the person is ailing, but alive. I come from two cultures which have much the same values. Please give yourself some time to come to terms with what is happening in your life, in the here and now. Stop motoring ahead, planning the future and missing out on some memorable moments.' Patience rattled on as she picked at her food, losing the enthusiasm she felt a minute ago. Felicity, headstrong and insensitive as usual did not pick up the cue to stop.

'It does make my western thoughts seem callous, don't you think? And it's me wanting to always organise things ahead of time, as I do. I know I come across as a control freak, but it's just the way I am. How do I begin to change that at this stage of my life?'

'No, you're not callous – just different to how I view life and death. Slow down. What I know about being callous is Mrs Beresford's daughter, whose busy life kept her from coming to Australia to see her ill mother or attend her funeral. How do daughters cast their mothers out in their time of need? That is what I take issue with!'

'Yes, I remember the letter from the high and mighty parliamentarian.'

Patience nodded in remembrance of the cold letter from June Beresford De Vaal.

'These are the lessons we learn every day, and we should be grateful for being the way we are. We are never too old, nor too young to be told that we need to learn a better way.'

'It's more me, than you, Patience, I can have my give-a-damn moments but you're too nice to point them out to me, but I take cognisance of what you're saying. I have lessons to learn, I will try,' she whispered.

Patience noted the change in Felicity's consideration of her attitude to life. She perceived the beginnings of a mellowed sensitivity that she enjoyed seeing in her friend. Grace would be pleased with this change.

MUCH AWAITED her in Sydney as Grace came to terms with the next challenge in her personal world.

7

COMPLICATIONS

The return flight from Melbourne had Patience wondering whether she should call Masuyo as requested. She was eager to get back into the swing of things at her SHSO office. The number of women seeking protection from domestic violence at their centre had increased by at least thirty-five percent, making another safe house necessary. The nature and extent of the violence urged the opening of a house away from the metropolitan district, to perhaps country New South Wales.

Sydney airport thronged with hurried exits and entrances. People consumed with where they were headed, wanting to get ahead in the queue. For a fleeting second, she yearned for the peace, and wide spaces at the Mission. She ignored overthinking that, her purpose was to serve what came to her. Thoughts on whether Akanya could have been kidnapped and held hostage, mounted. Was her involvement with the Mission known in broader circles around India? She flinched, reminded of Lindiwe's deliberate media faux pas.

Power infiltrated every aspect of society, some, although limited, were for valid reasons in bringing about universal change, on issues of racism, sexism, ageism, and basic human rights. Others were vainglorious, feeding private and insane pursuits. She contemplated whether South Africa and the United States would see a female leader soon, or India another female Prime Minister.

On a whim she asked her taxi driver to re-route her destination. She had an urgent need to be in her own home. Hiding from the pressure the media might create was not going to rule her every day decisions. Her drive from Karachi with Akbar's driver came flooding back with her encounters with Balthazar, Maimoona, and the handsome Azmil at the Well Study Centre. She felt a yearning to know how they were doing. Pakistan stirred her soul in a way she had not expected. The emotional chord struck in unlikely places, and disquieted the soul, making the return there, a deep-seated desire. Azmil was a selfless soul working in memory of his mother's pain, her lost love, lost family life, and never getting to know him. If every son showed such profound love for his mother, many would be free of tears.

Deep stirrings jolted back to reality with the GPS announcement, 'Arrived!' In a panicked moment, she asked the driver to take a slow ride around the block before she got out the car.

'Are you sure, madam? It will be at an extra cost, you know.'

'Yes, I am sure. Please drive until I tell you when to stop. I will pay the extra time on the clock, not to worry.'

'If you are afraid of something, I can call the police, or 000, just say the word, madam. Are you in some sort of danger? I need to know.'

'No such thing! I'm taking in the scenic view of the neighbourhood after being away for such a long time.'

'I see. Did you have a nice holiday? Where did you travel?'

The driver's questioning distracted her. She scanned the local landscape expecting to see the media in waiting for her, ready to pounce.

'I did, thank you. I'm returning from Melbourne, but I was in Pakistan, not so long ago. You can stop now.'

'Pakistan? That is my home country? Oh wow, madam!'

Patience opted not to respond to stop further personal questions being asked. She got off the car, grabbed her bags and hurried into her home. Ajax and Sprite whimpered when they picked up her scent, peering in through the patio doors to get a glimpse of her.

After a couple of hours of dog-baby heaven, pampering the two joys in her life, washing away the guilt for having left them again, she heard her mobile phone ringing in the kitchen.

'Patience, where are you? I've been sick with worry.' Grace wheezed down the phone. Her asthma surfaced with stress.

'Gracie! Sorry! I'm here with Sprite and Ajax. I meant to stop for a brief stay and got carried away by the oodles of love they've showered on me!' She laughed her husky laugh that comforted Grace with the knowledge that her sister was safe and well.

'Thank God! I had visions that the media bombarded you at the airport and you were held for questioning! My overactive imagination, as usual!'

'I was on high alert, from the minute I landed, because I had that fear too! The poor taxi driver must have thought I was on drugs!'

'Stay put. I'm coming to you with dinner tonight. Let Virginia know the sisters are bombarding her peace, and she is invited to share dinner with us.'

She hung up before Patience could object. Virginia was delighted that Grace was coming over and insisted that she would bring a home-made dessert for an after-dinner treat. With dinner plans set, Patience tossed her phone on her bed to avoid any distractions as she devoted more time to pampering Ajax and Sprite. They had a larger box of toys that Virginia had spoilt them with, as she too felt guilty about her long days at the SHSO office. Playing fetch, running around the backyard, enjoying some freedom helped her connect with her inner child. For once, she did not have to think beyond the moment, secluded in her backyard.

Grace arrived at 7 pm with the pungent aroma of Goan fish curry and pickles. She hugged Patience with the same fervour as if she had just returned after a long absence.

'Sorry to have you in a frenzy with not letting you know my whereabouts. I was cautious in not using my phone, lest the media fiends were on my tail.'

'I understand. Tell me how Felicity and Alf are doing. We won't bore Virginia with these details, so let's chat before she gets in from work.'

Grace who was always considerate, understood that someone as young as Virginia, need not be bogged down by talk of illness, ageing and dying. She was young, yet sensible and sensitive to the pain of others. This made her much-loved by the women in the safe houses. They could talk to her with the assurance that she understood their pain.

'Can we also talk about the missing Indian lady, later in the evening?'

'Yeah, I don't have any further updates on her. Does this mean you're staying over tonight? Please say, *yes*.'

Grace heard the child in Patience's request, and although she had no intention of sleeping over, she agreed.

'I will, if you share a set of pj's with me!' Grace laughed.

'I have a new set stashed away for you, in preparation for your unplanned stay. Its party night, let's put on some smooth grooves, I have a bottle of white in the fridge.'

'Right on time, that sounds like Virginia at the door.'

PATIENCE NOTICED that as the evening drew on, Grace appeared distracted. She slipped into long spells of silence, unaware that she was twirling the ends of her hair. It could be exhaustion, or perhaps something troubled her that she could not hide for too long? Intuition told her something far more serious, than Grace was prepared to admit, had unsettled her.

It was good to have time together, alone, after Virginia retired for the night. A sponsor wanted to meet regarding a new safe house, and she had to be well-rested for that. Her persuasive skills saved the organisation money which Patience was not successful in doing. She lacked bargaining skills, giving in to get the job done. Unlike her name, she was not prepared to wait for things to happen when women were in dire need.

'I'm blessed to have Virginia running the SHSO office and have you to thank for bringing her to us.'

'Fate had its way. I am happy to see her flourish in this role. You have been a godsend to her.'

'Felicity was amazed at her transformation, in coping on her own. Lindiwe has been of great help to her too.'

'I'm glad that Felicity has changed her thinking on Virginia. So, are you serious about keeping Lindiwe on?'

'Well, she's aware she's under scrutiny, and time will tell. She needs the job, I believe she won't slip up again.'

Grace gave no indication that she wanted to broach what troubled her. Patience's, *tell me all, tell me now,* instinct kicked in.

'Grace, it's no secret that something is on your mind. I caught you curling your hair!. You made quite a knot at one point! You must speak up. Let us not repeat the past. We need each other.'

'Oh, Patience! You know me better than I know myself, some-times. Are you up to listening to my troubles?'

'Absolutely! A problem shared is a problem halved, right?'

Grace nodded, her brown eyes darkened, she hunched over.

'Keefe's session with Dr Deakin ended up with her telling him he had to be upfront with me, even if he thought I would be hurt by it.'

'Has he not been honest about something?' Patience was irritated by the thought and afraid for Grace.

'Something new surfaced, during his session, that he found difficult to raise with me after all the issues that followed his mam's passing.'

Grace avoided eye contact, she began to sway in her seat, perturbing Patience that something terrible had happened.

'Is the ex-wife demanding something else now?'

'No, this is something entirely different. It seems...' she broke off with a deep sigh, '... it seems Keefe has a four-year-old child from another woman.'

Patience shook her head in disbelief, 'You can't be serious!'

'Well, there's a story, every man has one, I suppose. He told me everything, the day we spent together. Now, I have big decisions to make. I am so confused, Patience. I need your objective opinion, not what you kindly assume is good for me.' Her pleading eyes revealed she was drowning in her search for a solution.

'I promise to do that. As much as I want Keefe to be in your life, I will not accept him hurting you with untruths. If he has, then he must leave now.'

'Not untrue, just afraid with this new information arising, after we returned from his mam's funeral in Belfast.'

'This is killing me, I hate to say it, but please explain.'

'He received a letter from a lawyer in Spain, asking for a DNA test as the child's mother has named him as the father. She has ovarian cancer and can't care for the child anymore.'

'My goodness, Grace! You had me thinking it might be confirmed! How, when, where did this happen?'

'He admitted to having a one-night stand on the last night after a conference in Spain, but says he was drunk at the time and his memory is hazy.'

'Swine! They all say that when they're caught out! Do you believe this? I have a few charming words to define what I think!' Patience stood up, irritated, this was too close to the struggles of the women at her safe houses.

'I told him to have the DNA test, and to face whatever it is with responsibility for his actions. I will not be with a man who denies his child the right to his father who is alive and well. I don't care how the child came to be in the world. The adults are responsible to provide care and love.'

'Are you saying, this won't end your relationship with Keefe?'

'I can't say what I think, at this stage. It depends on his actions. Lord above, these challenges know how to find me!' She covered her face and peered through the gaps of her fingers to observe her sister's reaction.

'You are sensible in not overreacting. Will he have to go to Spain for the DNA test?'

'We have not figured that one out yet. He's still reeling from the surprise that he might be the father of a four-year-old little boy.'

'Whatever your decision is, I am right here behind you, you know that. Take it one day at a time. Don't turn your back on him, let him do the test and decide what you want to do. You owe it to yourself to take care of your inner world first. You need a good night's sleep, so I suggest you do that now.'

Patience had to be direct with Grace to ensure she did not neglect her own mind, body and spirit. She would be called upon to deal with much more in the days ahead.

THAT NIGHT PATIENCE picked up her phone to find several missed calls from Ming with no voicemail or text messages left.

8

INDIA CALLING

Patience tossed and turned, guilty that she did not return Ming's multiple missed calls. The signs were there, her life was about to be tested again. Her only consolation was that nothing could be worse than being held prisoner at the chief's kraal in South Africa and being a concubine to a man old enough to be her great-grandfather.

She promised to go book hunting with Grace, the next morning, now all she wanted was more sleep. Keefe's motivational book search could not be canceled. A major part of her acknowledged, with pleasure, that Grace was trying to fix her relationship with Keefe.

They arrived at Abbey's Bookshop on York Street, and spent an hour browsing around the shelves.

'You could have checked online first before coming to the bookshop, you know.'

'I know, but I need to look for other books too. What better way than to see, touch and experience the book you've wanted for so long. I love the smell of new books. And besides I look forward to a chat with the friendly staff here.'

'No doubt, the therapeutic value of walking through a book-shop, browsing and purchasing a book is not to be denied.'

Patience remembered their childhood trips to the Long Market Street library in South Africa. She was an unwilling reader, back in the day. It took a banana milkshake bribe to get her to accompany Grace on her Saturday morning visits to the library. Soon she was hooked on reading Enid Blyton's *Noddy,* and the *Nancy Drew* series. Then there were trips to CNA, the newsagents, to grab Grace's favourite British magazine, *Blue Jeans.* At the time, she did not appreciate the value of her sister's Saturday morning book and magazine tradition. She loved to chat to any willing person, while Grace locked herself away in her introverted world, engrossed in the lives of the characters in the books she read. Pen-pals were the craze of the day, and thirteen-year-old Grace from South Africa, had scores of English and Irish pen-pals who wanted to befriend her. Soon she chose two, both named Janet, one from England, the other from Ireland. After many years of writing to each other, she lost contact with both.

'Watching you page through your darling books, was a journey across time for me. Now I'm drooling for that milkshake!'

'Oh, Patience, those were lovely days, and how lucky are we to still be doing this. You should read again. You seem to have dropped the habit in recent years. You will be surprised when you find yourself between the pages of a novel.'

'I agree. There's a book for everyone. I've stacked them up on my bedside table and intend to get to them soon.'

Grace recalled Patience's ingenious excuses for not having read the books she recommended during their high school years.

'No excuses, you have some time to yourself now with Virginia's assistance at the SHSO office.'

'True.'

A leisurely morning and high tea at QVB topped the day for both. They had this time in the tea-house to pretend to be relaxed, pampered Victorian women.

On the car ride home Patience made a note to return Ming's call.

'I should call Masuyo first, for the latest update, and Ming later today.'

'Something must be amiss with so many calls from Ming. You should return her call as a matter of urgency.'

'Yeah, I should have called her for updates before I left for Melbourne. I will do so after my call to Masuyo.'

'Think before you commit to anything, this time.' Grace looked at her sister to gauge her reaction.

'I will,' was Patience's soft reply.

THE CALL TO MASUYO, after hesitating at first as it was close to midnight in New York, resulted in Patience sending a text message that she thought was not as invasive at that hour. Masuyo called her right away.

'Truth, Understanding and Compassion greetings to you, sister Patience.'

Patience was quiet for a second. TUC was absent from her lips and mind ever since she returned. Her head spun with the awkward realisation that she had not carried the greeting with her, it was the basis of the Mission's ideology for a New World Order.

'Hi Masuyo the same to you. How are you? I apologise for not getting back to you sooner. I was away in Melbourne for the weekend.'

Guilt for not returning the TUC greeting made her hesitate. She could not bring herself to continue with the greeting in a place where she would be considered odd, or part of a cult for doing so. Did that really matter, had she not moved away from caring about what others thought of her? Whatever happened to being authentic?

She asked how Zuri, Xandria and Alexis were doing.

'They are well and send their greetings to you. They are here in New York with me. Have you had any news from Ming?' Masuyo gave nothing else away, keeping to business as she always did.

'No, I will call her soon. How have things progressed with the Mission and the new leadership recruits?'

'Mission work continues like clockwork. Sadly, very sadly, I must tell you that Sister Akanya has passed away. We have no idea how or why.'

Patience put the phone down on the kitchen counter for a second. Her heart thundered, and a deep sadness gripped her. She forced herself to pick up the phone with trembling hands, her mind in a daze.

'This is a shock. I am so sorry to hear this. I don't understand what has happened.'

'We are just as shocked, here. You grew close to sister Akanya while you were in training.'

'Yes, I did, as did Ming. Do you have any idea how and why this has happened?'

'We are ignorant as to how she died. The only thing we know is that her body was found on the side of the Taj Expressway. It's unclear whether it was a motor vehicle accident.'

Patience ached inside for Akanya who had escaped so many atrocities in her life – now dead, and nobody had any answers. How could this happen? She lived her life to the letter of the law, proud of her cultural heritage, and the land of her birth.

'Dear God, this is the worst news I've had since my return to Australia. Where to from here?'

'Yes, it has left us all deeply saddened. Please speak to Ming, she needs support too. She is our gentle one. I do also have another request.'

Patience closed her eyes, unsure of what she was going to be asked to do, and whether she had the willpower to refuse this time around.

'Can you meet, Alexis and Xandria in India, to assist Ojala, Akanya's second in charge with the funeral arrangements? All I need is for you to be there to watch over, instruct and coordinate the proceedings. I don't envisage any problems. We want our sister laid to rest with the dignity she deserves.'

Patience felt the weight of a hundred angels pressing down on her. Akanya's dead? Decisions? Choices? Funeral arrangements?

'One more thing, I will also need the next leader put in place to head the centre there. Ojala Diya is very young, but I could be wrong, she might be willing and capable to pick up the reins.'

She had to think quickly, before the requests increased. Masuyo flogged a willing and able horse. She had carefully planned and executed her request, no doubt appealing to compassion to guide Patience's decision.

'I need some time to think about this, with my responsibilities at the SHSO office. We have many new projects in the pipeline that require my undivided attention.'

True to Masuyo as she had come to understand her, she listened to only what she needed expedited.

'I need an answer within twenty-four hours. Whatever you need, let us know.'

'Thank you. I will be in touch, once I can figure out how I will manage my office while I'm away. What time frame are we talking, here?'

Masuyo sighed with relief, knowing that this was a sign that Patience would not fail her. She delivered on everything the Mission hurled at her.

'At least two weeks, I would say. One week for the funeral arrangements, provided there are no issues, and one week to set up the leader there.'

'I will call you tomorrow. Truth, Understanding and Compassion be with you.' No sooner had she said it, she was drawn back into the fold. Akanya, poor Akanya made sure she did not stay removed for too long.

The call to Ming was a quick one, she was devastated, but determined to get to India in a day or two to assist Ojala.

'We are distressed with this news. Can you imagine what Ojala is going through? I won't rest until I know I can be of assistance. Poor Akanya, I hope she did not suffer too much.'

'Who knows, Ming, who knows? I might call Ojala to find out if more has come to light.' They parted with heavy sadness.

How could she go to India when Grace needed her emotional support with all that had happened in Keefe's life? Then there was Andrew, still somewhat recovering from his appendectomy. He was back on shift at ER but had to have extra days off to recover after a hectic night. Virginia coped with all her duties but Lindiwe Johnson had a shady side. India was calling on a matter of grave importance. Akanya deserved a grand send-off. Patience had many balls to juggle. How could she accomplish everything that was coming her way? She had to let Grace know that she might be leaving again, soon. Virginia would have to be sworn to secrecy to ensure that Lindiwe kept away from the media or did not give in to temptation in revealing anything when they called. She abhorred secrets and was sickened by the thought that she had to adopt this approach with her SHSO staff!

Patience waited until morning to tell Grace the latest news. She was on shift that evening, she sent a text message asking Grace to come over to her place for breakfast. She baked a large batch of bran muffins.

'The best part of having you home, is that I have two homes to come to after a hectic night at work!' Grace glowed, she had put on a kilo or two, and enjoyed her sister's surprise treats. Patience on the other hand, shuddered that she was about to burst her sister's bubble. She was not going to skirt around the issue. She must say what had to be said and then hold her breath for her sister's response. Dancing around what she had committed to would mean she was not true to her intention.

'You could not have had any bran muffins while I was away, so

I woke up early and made you a fresh batch. My one and only signature baking skill!'

'Yum, just what I need this morning! No doubt my girth is expanding, but I cannot pass up having a few of these.'

'No sister of mine is going to look like a famine has struck. Our mothers will turn in their graves at that thought.'

'Keefe has not had any of your delightful muffins, so I will pack him a few, and I might see Andrew later this afternoon, he loves your muffins. I hope you don't mind me grabbing so many.'

'Not at all! Ja, it's the South African way, sis! Padkos!' Grace laughed when Patience said this. Her mother packed a take home parcel for all her visitors including scones for the awkward Anton Wessels.

'Grace, you have too many men in your life! Take them all, I really should not be having any more muffins!'

The souls of Varuna's and Elsie's daughters were as steadfast in their bond to each other from the first day they met. Two sisters from different cultural backgrounds lived under the divided sky of apartheid. Patience had to work her way into saying what she had to.

'Any news, yet, on Keefe's DNA test?'

'Yes, he can be tested here, without going to Spain, not yet anyway.'

'Do you think he will go at some point?'

'Yeah, I'm prepared for that possibility. Keefe seems to think he won't have to go.'

'How does he explain that?'

'He can't, not yet. I believe the mother would not have dug him up, if she was not sure that he was the father. She is ill and the child's future hangs in the balance. She must be a good woman. She left him out of it for four years, now it's necessary that she looks to the best option for the boy.'

'Time is the test, I suppose. I'm glad you're being strong about this.'

She believed that Grace would accept the child, without a doubt, as Keefe's son. She had softened towards Keefe, since Patience returned. This new-found truth gave her a reason to understand his irrational behaviour. She too, valued knowing the truth, no matter how painful it was. Grace surprised her, with her positive reaction to Masuyo's request that she should go to India to pay homage to Akanya.

'I'm not surprised the Mission called upon you to join the group in India. It is a tragedy that has struck one of their own. I would not expect anything else other than that her friends and colleagues would rally together to send her off in love and peace.'

Grace was always practical, seeing into the sense of things. The decision now rested squarely on her shoulders.

'Thank you for understanding. I have twenty-four hours, now it's probably sixteen to eighteen hours to respond. Ming has committed to going.'

Life's tests came from any angle, often unpredicted. Changes were already in process for Grace, but as sisters, honour and compassion was their tour de force as the legacy their mothers had inculcated.

It was indeed *the best of times, the worst of times,* as Charles Dickens rightfully declared in *The Tale of Two Cities.*

9

VIRGINIA'S NEWS

The time had come for Virginia to give Patience her bit of news. She held off in the flurry of Patience's return, and Lindiwe's transgression. When Patience requested an off-site meeting, something serious was about to be announced. The rule, while Virginia lived at Patience's home, was that no work would be discussed after office hours.

Both lived under the emotional and psychological pressure in their line of work. They empathised with the harrowing domestic issues the women at the safe houses struggled with which often left them emotionally fatigued. They dodged irate husbands and boyfriends and cried quiet tears for the multitude of broken women who turned up at their SHSO door.

Patience had to be honest in all matters with Virginia to hold her trust as someone who was dedicated to the organisation's ethos. She could be trusted not to divulge her whereabouts. Lindiwe's inability to know when to remain silent was a bone of contention for Patience. She was nervous that Virginia had an offsite meeting with the boss.

'I hate to sound like a scratched vinyl. Is this meeting about my dismissal? I get really stressed when you both meet outside the office.'

'Patience would have said so. This has nothing to do with your position, so keep calm.' She sympathised that a woman in her mid-fifties felt dispensable in a society that castigated her to the retired basket when she had many more working years left. Her experience guided Virginia in matters that needed an older ear.

'The media interviewed a German and a Swede, I think, a few weeks prior to her return. I don't know why she says it's classified information.' Lindiwe stopped when Virginia looked at her and took a deep breath. If she got on the wrong foot with her, it meant she had no support when Patience was on the war path.

'Patience is an ethical woman, you have to understand that. I work here, because her head and heart are in the right place. She will do things her way, I suggest you keep out of what does not involve your work here at our SHSO.'

'Sorry... I did not mean to... yes got it... I won't... '

Virginia left without another word.

Patience waited for her at The Restaurant Pendolino, for some refined dining to soothe her troubled soul. Virginia was out of her comfort zone in formal settings, unsure of the social etiquette. Patience relaxed, comfortable in her skin unlike her sister and Virginia who were flustered when they perceived watchful eyes.

'You need to relax, Virginia, you work too hard. How are things at the office?'

'All good, thanks. Lindiwe's edgy about our meeting, she thinks it's about her possible dismissal.'

Patience laughed off Lindiwe's uneasy speculations. She was comforted by Virginia's genuine concern over Akanya's passing, but what she had not anticipated or suspected was Virginia's hurried disclosure.

'I hope to move into my apartment in a week or so, and my

partner will spend weekends with me. You need your space at home, as do I. Don't get me wrong, I appreciate everything you've done for me and continue to do.'

Patience understood this young woman's need to find her place in the world. Personal space was necessary in a new relationship.

'Is everything going well with your grandmother? Has she settled in at the nursing home?' Patience held back asking about the 'partner' that Virginia casually mentioned.

'She is well and loves it there. I am not much of a conversationalist. She enjoys the company and activities at the place.'

'You do know there is no pressure to leave my place. You can do so whenever you want.'

'I know, thank you... the man I'm dating... and I, are not in any hurry to commit to marriage, not just yet, but we want to spend more time together.'

'How have you managed to keep this relationship under wraps?'

'I'm not sure if you will... take issue with this. I met him through the SHSO, he is one of the sponsors for the country safe house.'

Patience searched her memory for who it could be but avoided a guess.

'Who is it? I don't have any issue with you meeting someone through our SHSO. You spend many hours of your life at work, it makes sense that you will meet a soul-mate this way.'

Virginia appreciated her calm understanding. Patience treated her like family, not an employee, she was part of the organisation, and valued for her contributions. She had heard of the struggles of some women working in situations where they were mistreated, not allowed to have a say, had to work long hours and were poorly paid.

'Moran Vincento,' Virginia said in a soft voice as she searched Patience's face for her reaction.

'Really? I would never have guessed, but then again, I haven't been around much in recent months.'

'I am the happiest I have ever been in a long time. He is caring, attentive and loving. The age-gap is not an issue at all.'

Patience reached across to squeeze Virginia's hand when she saw her brim with happiness.

'Congratulations! You deserve a good man to care for you. You have my blessings, and I know Grace will be overjoyed too.'

'I hope so.'

'Absolutely, she will be, guaranteed! What time-frame do you have for your plans?'

'Moran will only be over at the apartment with me from Friday to Sunday night. He will stay at his home in Rosebay during the week.'

'No, I did not mean your personal arrangements. I meant tying the knot. You said not just yet, but is this in the offing sooner rather than later? I need early notice with the way my life seems to be going!' Patience chuckled.

'Moran is keen to marry soon. He's been alone for the last ten years since his wife passed away. I want to wait a bit.'

'Good on you for not rushing into things! You, Grace and I should have a celebratory dinner together. Does Lindiwe know about Moran?'

'No way! I wanted you to be the first to know. Moran will tell his children this week. They are adults with their own busy lives. His youngest son is involved in the business with him. I am a little nervous about what they will say when they realise the age difference.'

'I am sure he is a sensible man and will handle things with his children. Really, they don't have a say in his happiness at all, you know.'

Virginia relaxed, then asked to know more about the organisation in India.

'I have yet to find out who will be present from the Mission and what the expectations are. I have to let them know today if I am going over.'

'Surely, you are going? You said you were close to the Indian and Chinese delegates, and an American, if I remember this correctly.'

'Yes, that's right, I survived the situation because of their friendship.'

'Let your compassion guide you, and don't worry about things here, I will hold the fort for you.'

'I know, thank you. I will tell you more about Akanya soon. Her life story, and ability to move on with her life with no hatred, is something I will never forget.'

Patience's capacity to see the value in others when she herself was a role-model of strength and compassion, is what Virginia hoped to emulate.

'I should come back to the office with you, to calm Lindiwe's nerves.' Patience giggled.

GRACE'S obvious excitement when she heard Virginia's news, pleased Patience. Her sister had the ability to ignore her problems in order to celebrate the joy of others.

'I am super happy for her. She deserves love in her life. I don't mean to sound crass, but with the age difference, she is more likely to remain committed to the organisation. It's younger men that demand more of a woman's time and attention.'

'It's up to her. I won't stand in her way if she chooses to opt out from her SHSO role.'

'I doubt she will. She has found her calling with this job.'

'I hope so.'

'Happiness governs all facets of life. Now, have you booked your trip with India calling?'

'Yeah, I will today. Virginia is happy to cover for me while I'm away, but I haven't confirmed anything with Masuyo yet.'

Grace's tone confirmed that Patience had her approval.

'I'm glad that you've made the decision to go to India. You will be miserable forevermore if you don't attend to what matters to you.'

'Thank you so much. Are you going to be okay with Keefe's matters?'

'I have resigned myself to the fact that Keefe is the father and will support that.'

'That's love talking, Gracie! I will be gone for two weeks, not too long.'

'Let's not count the days. We can chat about your experience, while you are there. If it wasn't for Keefe's current situation, and Andrew's slow healing, I would have jumped at the opportunity to go to India with you.'

'There will be another time. It would be amazing to have your support on this trip, but duty calls, I understand.'

On that note Patience called Masuyo, she was thankful for her rearrangement of her own work commitments to help with Akanya's funeral. She knew Patience would not fail her. Zuri waited in anxious anticipation with her mother for Patience's response.

'I knew I could count on sister Patience, she is a perfect soul, kanpekina tamashī, as my mother used to say.'

Zuri interlocked her palms and sighed in relief.

The next few days were spent at the SHSO office, Patience assisted Virginia to complete most tasks in preparation for setting up the country safe house. Remote access to the SHSO portal was on her agenda, to allow Virginia time to look after her relationship with Moran Vincento.

That night Grace curled up in a foetal position on her couch, enveloped in the soft folds — all their lives were changing, they had to go with the ebb and flow.

Everything happened for a reason is what she had to believe.

10

COLOURFUL CULTURE

On Wednesday morning Patience arrived in India. Ming, Xandria and Alexis arrived a day earlier.

The heat sucked the air from her lungs. She was used to intense summers in Australia but had to brace herself for a different intensity.

The Mission arranged all her transportation from flights and a pre-booked taxi. She was stormed by a group of taxi drivers of varying ages, turbaned, long-haired, bearded, smiling, and eager to secure business.

'Where does madam want to go? I will do half-price fare, just for you.'

Faces bobbed around her, and with the added heat she felt faint.

'I have a taxi booked, thank you.'

This did not deter their persistent requests. Palms raised above their heads in mocked reverence made her guilty for having a pre-booked taxi. She was warned to avoid being lured by requests for better deals that her big heartedness would unwittingly invite.

After ten minutes, Sultan arrived with a placard with her

name with the 'e' before the 'i'. She fell into his air-conditioned car and eagerly reached for the chilled bottled-water he offered her. This was an upmarket vehicle and service. The Mission spared no expense to get her here with all the comforts she needed. Sultan was silent, he smiled and nodded when she asked a question. She figured he either had limited understanding of English, was nervous in company, or perhaps an introvert. She settled in her comfortable seat and dozed off for the long drive ahead.

SHE ARRIVED IN BALMY PANNA. Perspiration rolled down her back the instant she stepped out of the air-conditioned car. Beads of sweat popped above her eyebrows, upper lip and chin. She was desperate for a shower and change of clothes. The air was heavy with the perfume of incense. She thanked Sultan who refused a tip.

'No, no, madam, they paid me.'

Here again was another surprise, he spoke English after all, and was an honest man.

A tall, slim, young woman approached her from a narrow, lit path alongside the building in front of her. With clasped palms and bowed head, she introduced herself.

'I am Ojala Diya, we spoke on the telephone. Welcome to our humble school and home. You must be exhausted, sister.'

She looked no older than the young women she had worked with in Pakistan. Akanya told her that Ojala came to her after she had escaped a brutal arranged marriage. She was reliable and passionate in serving their community of students.

Patience returned the clasped palm, bowed head greeting. She admired Ojala's youthful freshness.

'Great to meet the lovely you behind the voice. How are you holding up?'

'Holding up?' Ojala's perplexed look confirmed that she had

to speak with specific choice of vocabulary to eliminate any misunderstanding. Her sense of humour would have to be kept in check too.

'How are you coping after Akanya's passing?'

'I am coping, but I miss her so much. It's like my arms, legs and soul are missing. We still don't know why this happened or who did this to her. Come, we should go inside, everybody is waiting to meet you.'

Patience reached out to hug Ojala. She clung to her needing the comfort of the embrace. A bony frame beneath her diaphanous cotton pants and long top made Patience release her tight grip. Ojala's world had collapsed in a matter of days. She had to pick up, and possibly lead from where Akanya stopped.

A simple wood-and-iron classroom was at the front of the property. The place was familiar from Akanya's proud, detailed description of her technology school. The residential quarters were further behind the school, packed in a tight cluster of individual rooms with one large communal kitchen and dining area.

Patience noticed the ceiling fans. No air conditioner! She would have to acclimatise soon if she was to be of any assistance to Ojala during her time here. Another young woman welcomed her with a tall chilled glass of mango juice. She gulped it down with gratitude when Grace's warning voice echoed in her head.

Do not drink any liquid that is not bottled, please, if you don't want to be hospitalised. Grace's last words when she left, stung her ears now. She had to make a conscious effort to refuse ice in her drinks. Crunching ice was her summertime treat, but not while she was in India.

Ojala introduced the young woman, Hiyana, as her helper while she was at the centre.

She protested that she did not need a helper, when she realised it might be construed as an insult. Ojala stared at her in wide-eyed disbelief.

'Please, Kanya-Ma would want you to have Hiyana as your assistant, to help you navigate around language and culture.'

Her perception of what Indian culture was in South Africa was different to what it was like here, in its unassimilated essence.

'In that case, I thank you and am happy to have Hiyana guide me around.'

'It will be totally my pleasure to be your guide, madam. Thank you for accepting. Awesome!' Hiyana's flawless, lilting English tones reminded Patience of Jane Austen's characters, except for the forceful use of 'awesome'!

Exotic India, the land of contrasts, infused her spirit. Generosity, humility, simplicity, and even the harassment from the taxi drivers made India intriguing. Hiyana's hand gesture when she said, 'totally,' was uncanny in its similarity to Akanya's gestures.

Akanya had a western head when she chose to, but her adherence to culture and values was strong. Varuna and Grace embraced a fusion of culture which was more anglophile than distinctly South African. Varuna's insistence on respect, good manners and a close check on appropriate behaviour was enforced in her childhood home.

MING, Alexis and Xandria were seated in the dining room, waiting for her. After a brief reunion of hugs, Patience asked if Zuri and Masuyo were arriving soon.

'They won't be coming to India.' Alexis said.

'Why?' Patience asked, confused with how she was coerced to attend Akanya's last rites when Masuyo had no intention of coming to India.

'New projects have surfaced, and she needed to attend to them. Zuri will not leave her mother alone with these pressures.'

Patience chose to stop asking further questions when she sensed the cover-up. There was no closeness between her, Alexis and Xandria – they were aloof, and businesslike. She hoped she was not expected to share a room with either of them. Two weeks in a tight space with them would be unbearable.

Ming's usual look of caution told her to stop delving for reasons.

'Does anybody have more information on how this awful situation occurred?'

'Nothing, the police came by earlier, and wanted to see Akanya's room, and left us with no new information.' Ming said.

'Foul play is a certainty, not just an accident as we thought earlier, especially with Akanya's brother Biddhu's body being found on the banks of the Ken.'

'Oh yes, I agree. That is so sad, brother and sister, gone forever.' Hiyana added.

Hiyana's sensitivity credited her in Patience's book. She spoke from the heart, and with fearless confidence on police apathy on the case.

Ming, Alexis and Xandria were allocated a young man, named Deepak, to assist them. He melted Patience with his disarming smile and eagerness to please. Ojala, Hiyana and Deepak served a simple dinner of rice, cumin potatoes and cauliflower in a watery yoghurt sauce. Hiyana explained that because Akanya was Hindu, they were serving vegetables during the mourning period. She added that after the funeral they would serve meat dishes to the visitors.

Patience was the first to protest, 'I am sure we are all happy to remain vegetarian while we are here as your guests, and as our mark of respect for dear Akanya.'

Nobody else protested. Alexis and Xandria excused themselves to retire for the night. Ming moved closer to Patience for a quiet word. Hiyana and Deepak cleared up the table and stood in the background to allow them the space for a private conversation.

Deepak offered to make a masala chai which Patience was

delighted to accept. Ming aired her distress through tears on Akanya's untimely death.

'She had so much more she wanted to do here. Life is so unfair. Alexis and Xandria know something that they're not sharing.'

'Nothing's changed from the Mission days, with the withholding of information. The conversation with them was strained.'

'Yes, I felt it too. I will stay on for the funeral and leave as soon as possible to get back to my school.'

'Yeah, so will I, but Masuyo asked that I help to set up a person to take over the reins from Akanya. Did she ask you too?'

'Where is she? Fine leader for not being here. She did ask, I told her I can't promise, I will see how things go while I'm here.'

'Ojala is capable to continue, all she needs is a second in charge. I am sure she can recommend someone. Hiyana looks like one with promise. What do you think?'

'I'm not thinking at all, I don't want to get involved, if I don't have to.'

'Fair enough, you must do whatever is best for you.'

They speculated whether brother and sister would be laid to rest together. Soon they retired to their rooms, it was well past midnight and the place was still abuzz with preparations for the next day. Patience was grateful for not having to share a room with anyone. She looked forward to a shower, all she could have at that hour was a cast-iron bucket bath, more like a swab. There were shower cubicles out in the yard — they had no electricity connected which made a night shower impossible.

Colourful India had already endeared itself to her, she was prepared to forgo some minor luxuries. The people, the location of Akanya's school, filled her with greater respect for the woman she at first judged for her uninvited mothering qualities, and eccentricities. It was only when she became aware of her life story during the personal testimony sessions that she was drawn to her in love and respect. She recalled Audra's criticism of the contradictions in India, and Akanya's vehement defence of her Motherland. Scoundrels were to be found, east, west, north and south of the globe. Here, in tranquil Panna she felt the spirit of Akanya watching over them.

She sent a text message to Grace who asked if she could call her for a chat.

'I'm glad you've settled in, already. The days ahead will be hectic leading up to the funeral.'

Patience sighed with exhaustion at the thought of the emotional journey she was yet to face.

'That's the thing, nothing has been arranged yet. The police are still snooping around, is what I've heard. I don't know how much help I'm going to be. This infernal heat is already leaving me restless.'

'Please check the cultural expectations and consult, consult, consult with the elders before you decide to do anything. Don't you have an air conditioner in your room?'

'I know, I will, but there are no elders on site to turn to for advice. I have a lovely assistant, a savvy young woman, who will point me in the right direction, I'm sure. Air conditioner? You kidding me?'

'Oh dear, I hope the heat subsides in the days ahead. Watch the water you drink. It's easy to slip up, so keep alert on that.'

'Yes, I am careful,' she lied and quickly asked, 'how are things with Andrew and Keefe?'

'Nothing more since you left, although Keefe gets the DNA results this week. He's been a bit morose. Story of my life these days!'

'Be gentle with him, Gracie. He's been through some hard times these past six months.'

'Yeah, but toughening up won't hurt, especially if he can't control what's already done.'

Patience added, 'You have the rest of your life to train him, so he'll be right!'

'At that distance, you will have a poke at me, little sis!' They laughed at Patience's unchanged liberty with her sister.

As Patience was about to turn over to sleep, she saw the screen of her phone light up. It was a text message from Akbar saying he was summoned to India to assist with the arrangements for Akanya's send-off. To the best of her knowledge, he had not met Akanya – Masuyo used her persuasive tactics to get her people over, while she remained ensconced in New York.

The Mission wilderness was an unfathomable one. Who were they really serving?

She hoped morning would bring more clarity on why Akanya had departed so soon. Now sleep was impossible with the heat of the night and morning just two hours away.

11

CHANGE OF HEART

Keefe's nervous wait for the DNA results was over.

It was confirmed — he was the biological father of a little boy somewhere in Granada. His earlier denial, and resistance that this could be remotely possible, came crashing down, leaving him caught between overwhelming sadness and joy. Memory returned with waves of guilt for the one-night, brief moments with the boy's mother, a university student working as a bartender. He tried to explain away his guilt as loneliness after his divorce, a hectic week at the conference and a friendly bartender who listened to his drunken woeful tales. Guilt opened the flood gates. For someone who upheld that emotions should be kept in check as a professional, he was as weak as a baby. Catholic guilt from his formative years resurfaced to question his sense of self-worth. He vaguely remembered the mother's face but had no recollection of her name. He left that night with no contact details and no intention of keeping in touch. His head hammered – how could I have done this? I left a child without a father for four years. I had no idea. Where do I even begin?

Grace hovered around in silence, allowing him the headspace to take it all in.

'This is good news, Keefe. Now you have confirmation, you can act accordingly. There's time, plenty of it for you to get to know your son. Be grateful that you discovered now, he's but a babe, not an adult that you would never have got to know.' She held his hands and peered into his face like a mother tending her injured child. Renewed tenderness surged when she saw him this way.

'Aye, thank you, for always understanding, mo ghrá. I have let you down, I won't blame you if you choose to leave me.'

'Don't be silly, why would I do that? We've been through so much in our short time together. How have you let me down? This situation occurred a long time ago.'

'I don't deserve you, not with all this happening. Mam said I was lucky to have found you, mo ghrá.'

'We are going to get through this together. Just don't keep any secrets – *that* will ruin us. I need to know, to be able to understand or decide, for that matter, if I want to be part of whatever is troubling you. The thing now is that you have to arrange to go over to meet the child.'

'Aye, that's the next step. I don't know if I am ready for a meeting yet. I promise not to withhold anything from you. You should get some sleep, you'll be exhausted on shift tonight.'

This was the endearing quality she fell in love with, his capacity to be considerate for others when he fought his own emotional pain. If he could remain sober like he had been in recent weeks, they had a second chance at a life together.

Grace stepped out onto the balcony for some air before her afternoon nap. She left him to think through his plans for his first meeting with his little boy, but felt a niggling annoyance that he appeared not ready to take that step, just yet. He had to do this on his own. She did not want to complicate anything that would mar his arrangements with the child's mother. The thought of the child living with them made her anxious and excited.

Keefe was lost his in thoughts when he heard his phone beep. A message from the attorney in Spain appeared on his screen. A photograph of a little boy popped up, he had flaming red hair, piercing blue eyes, and a heart-melting smile. He looked into his own eyes. A thud in the centre of his belly brought a fresh flood of emotions. With a slow release of air from his stifled lungs, he whispered, 'my boy.'

The attorney provided the mother's telephone number and details about the child. He urged Keefe to make a trip to Spain as soon as possible to meet Carlos Flores, his son, as his mother's condition had declined rapidly in recent days. He circled the image of the bright, happy face with his finger, repeating aloud, 'I'm so sorry... so very sorry... I will make it up to you, if it's the last thing I do in this life...'

Grace listened to him express his promise to his son. She tiptoed to the bedroom to allow him this private moment.

He sent his sister, Aileen, a message confirming the results and forwarded the photograph of Carlos to her. She called him immediately upon receiving the photo.

'He's a Daly, for sure. Aye, you can't miss that. He's gorgeous! Your boy is an adorable Irish-Spanish boy! How are you feeling, Keefe?'

'Overwhelmed and excited, a little muddled, I'm afraid.'

'I can understand that. Do you want me to come with you to see him when you make that trip to Spain?'

'Thank you, for that. Perhaps the first visit should be on my own. I'm not sure what I'm walking into regarding Camila. I just discovered her name now through the attorney. How pathetic am I, Aileen?'

Guilt made him wretched – he had failed his sister and Grace.

Aileen clicked her tongue on the other end of the line.

'Look you can't undo this, so being miserable and beating

yourself up, is worthless now. Gain strength to move on. Please stay away from the alcohol if you want Grace to trust you. How is she doing with this news?'

'You are right, as always. No alcohol, I made that promise. Grace is amazing, she wants me to do the right thing, and suggests that I go as soon as possible. She too, does not deserve this complication in her life.'

'She is a compassionate person, on the other hand Siobhan would have had a tantrum. You are blessed with Grace, you know.'

'I do know that, but please don't mention Siobhan again, please.'

'You rest now and decide by this evening when you plan to go to Spain.'

She hung up, leaving him hopeful that the two women who mattered the most in his life, second to his mam, had his back with no judgements leveled at him.

He crept into the bedroom and snuggled up to Grace.

His life had done a three-hundred-and-sixty degree turn in a matter of days.

THAT NIGHT, Grace arrived earlier than usual at City Hospital. A quick message to Andrew ensured he had coffee on the boil when he met her at the sliding doors to the Emergency Room. They walked into her office in knowing silence. Once away from inquisitive eyes, Andrew hugged her. He respected that she did not want a public show of affection between them at work. Nobody understood their friendship and unfounded speculations is what Grace wanted to avoid. Her privacy was sacrosanct.

'Lots to deal with now, Grace. How are you doing?'

It was a shock to her system finding out what had troubled and silenced Keefe, and his choice to drown his sorrows in too many bottles of whiskey. She processed pain with introspection, he blocked it.

'Yes, it is a lot to take in, but I feel the weight for Keefe. His emotions are raw.'

Her crinkled brow of consternation confirmed the weight she carried for Keefe. Her life, from the moment he was invited in, became an endless succession of challenges that tested her at every turn.

'Time is what he needs, what you both need really. Are you preparing for the fact that the child might live with Keefe, here in Australia?'

'Oh, Andrew, that is the right thing that should happen, and Keefe has to commit to that. I know in time he will. The thing is from what he says there isn't much time with the child's mother's health failing quite quickly.'

'I had no doubt that is how you would feel and what you would say on the matter. Leave it to him, look after you, for now.'

Grace understood Andrew's gentle advice – he witnessed all her highs and lows, from the therapy session with Dr Deakin that unlocked Boetie Arendse as her attacker to Patience going missing when her flight disappeared. She was stronger now than she had ever been, trust had developed in her key relationships which made her comfortable to talk about her challenges. Her biological clock did not promise that she would have her own child, perhaps this would be her destiny to motherhood. She contemplated all the reasons why she was enmeshed in this life situation, and accepted as her mother had taught her, to embrace what comes and to swim with it, not against it. She used a lovely analogy of the seashore of life and the churning of the tides, which she said soon passed, leaving radiant seashells as the treasures of life. Keefe was worth hanging onto as her life companion. He held the promise of a radiant seashell.

After many months, a quiet night fell over the Emergency Room leaving her the time to mull over recent happenings.

Andrew left her to her deep thoughts and caught up with the overflowing paperwork on his desk after his days off from his recent appendectomy.

BREAKFAST WAS ready for her when she got off shift that morning. Keefe announced that he had booked his flight to leave for Spain on Tuesday. More information had come to light, making him edgy. The child's mother had a partner who was living with her for the past two years. They did not have any children together.

'Apparently, for some reason, she won't say why she has not elected him as carer of the child while she's in the hospital. A friend is taking care of him.'

Grace listened with keen attentiveness.

'She has her reasons, which should not impact on your decision. I'm very happy that you are going over soon. I expect to be kept informed every step of the way. You don't want my anxiety going through the roof here,' she laughed. Her relief that he had committed to going to meet his son removed the deep crinkle from her brow.

'I will definitely do that. I need you to talk to, in helping me see the way forward. I need you to guide me. You, are more sensible than I will ever be.'

She tucked her arm in his, planted a resounding kiss on his troubled face and said, 'I don't know if I can be a guide, but a sounding board, yes, always. Sensible, sometimes, but I'm here.'

'That's all I need, mo ghrá.'

They spoke of the legal issues that might need attention. She reminded him to take all his documents that proved his identity and his residency in Australia. He had one week in Spain. If things were not finalised as the child's mother wished, he would have to return. He prepared himself for the event of anything coming up.

Grace's apartment or Keefe's one-bedroom pad close to the

hospital would not be ideal for raising a child. She had to proceed with one thought at a time. Her conversation with Patience significantly elevated her mood. Her joy about the possibility of having a child around them thrilled her.

'I am an Aunty! Can you imagine that! Wow, I'm excited for us! How about you, Gracie?' She tried to lower her voice, attempting to quell her excitement in a place of mourning.

Grace agreed that equal blessings and challenges would have to be embraced.

'Stop it, Grace, leave the practicalities out of it. Enjoy this moment. Deal with challenges when and if they do arise. Optimism, sis, remember that!'

She wished they could have more frequent girly chats. After Keefe went back to his place to gather his identity documents, she poured another cup of coffee and curled into her couch.

The joy in anticipating the arrival of a child came with the reminder that her life would never be the same again. She hoped she could deliver her promise to Keefe. With the unfolding of time, she learnt more about the suave, Dr Keefe Daly who tugged at her heartstrings in Amsterdam. She feared that there might be more secrets buried within the man she had tried to turn away from but failed.

Was his wild spirit tamed? Would he be a good father? Can she stay the course on this lifelong commitment with him? Thoughts swirled around her head preventing the usual snug sleep on her favourite couch.

12

INVESTIGATION

An uneasiness settled over the centre in Panna.

Police appeared every day, searching for something, expecting to pick up more clues. While they accepted that Akanya was murdered by the same criminals who killed her brother, they believed Akanya held the key to the reason for these gruesome acts.

None of them at the centre were her next of kin which shut them out from being privy to police findings. Police remained moustached, pursed-lipped and beady-eyed – a blockade of silence.

An official announcement confirmed that Akanya was strangled and Biddhu's death was by forcible drowning.

The reason underpinning both their deaths remained a mystery, leaving Patience confused as to why Masuyo requested that she assist in delaying Akanya's funeral.

Whenever the police turned up, unannounced, Deepak scurried to attention, Ojala kept away, locked in the school room or her bedroom. Hiyana followed them around like a puppy, eager to listen in to their conversations on her Kanya-Ma's brutal death.

As the slow wheels of Indian justice turned, Patience had to probe for what really happened for a sense of closure. It bothered her that Akanya obviously left in a hurry on the day she went missing, and yet the police chose not to clarify this.

She contacted Felicity to get more information on the retired Supreme Court judge to break through the police barrier. Insider contacts were the order of the day here. Felicity assured Patience that the lady would talk to her but making contact rested with her – the judge would not initiate the contact. She lived a distance away in picturesque Bangalore and ill health made traveling all the way to Panna impossible. Patience could not leave the centre during this crucial time. A telephone call would have to suffice as the way forward.

The judge warned her not to poke around too much, the police were a law unto themselves, if anyone, more especially a woman, asked too many questions. They could have her waiting months to years for answers. The retired judge's final comment was that Akanya's death was not an isolated incident. She said that it had something to do with her association with the recent work she did overseas. Patience pondered upon how much of the Mission's activity was common knowledge after all.

She walked to the rock garden that Ojala had told her offered a space for quiet thought. Coloured boulders of various sizes and shapes lined the footpath. Each boulder had an inspirational quotation inscribed in sculptured letters. This was the artwork of the young women at Akanya's centre. The first boulder, painted with glossy red paint, had the inscription:

No one really knows why they are alive until they know what they'd die for – Martin Luther King

Patience saw Akanya's legacy in those words. Even though she spoke out about matters that affected women in her country, there was a deep understanding that she spoke her truth with respect as her priority. This was the primary reason she clashed with the American woman, Audra, whose brazen criticisms of the East needed tempering. As she strolled down the footpath, the words of Mahatma Ghandi, Nelson Mandela and other human rights activists came into sight. The signpost at the end of the path was labeled, 'Contemplation Lane.' Akanya's influence was enduring, she had not only trained the young women in technological skills, she also opened their minds to equity and justice for all. Her mother's life of abuse as a widow, set her on this selfless path, as did her ruthless treatment at the hands of young army officers. A wooden bench at the end of the lane invited further contemplation, and soon thoughts of Grace emerged. A newcomer, a child in their lives would change their established worlds. The trickling of change was in motion, they had no option, but to embrace it.

A meeting with Alexis and Xandria was necessary. Ming busied herself by assisting Ojala with teaching the young women. She had to discuss, in privacy, the validity of the retired judge's speculations on the Mission in relation to Akanya's death.

After a cup of cardamom tea, she heard the police arrive, kicking up the dirt as they hurtled down the driveway of the centre, then came to a screeching halt covered in choking clouds of dense dust. It seemed police everywhere in the world had to make a grand entrance, hours after an emergency occurred. The incident with the dead black cat on their doorstep in South Africa was tossed aside, by a young police officer who arrived at top speed, three hours after the matter was reported. Then he had the audacity to insinuate that they were overreacting females! She put off seeing Alexis and Xandria to observe what the police were looking for, after their repetitive visits to the centre. She needed answers. In death there should be no secrets, Akanya's life deserved to be honoured not shrouded in secrets. Deep down she wanted confirmation that Akanya was not physically abused. She could not bear it if that was true. Akanya's personal testament left her in raw remembrance of what she had suffered through as a young woman, yet... she remained a smiling ray of hope for others. How does one experience and witness such violence and appear to remain unmarred as a kind, gentle, giving soul? These thoughts plagued Patience.

One police officer annoyed Patience the most. He twirled his thin, coiled moustache as he leered at Hiyana who stood too close to him, absorbed in wanting to hear everything. She had the urge to reprimand the policeman but remembered the judge's warning. All she could do was caution Hiyana and ensure that she was not left alone in the room with him. An older officer, perhaps in his mid-fifties, with a slight balding patch at the back of his head, a Deputy Inspector Manik Lal, looked at her and said, 'Sister Akanya Das is a victim of some vendetta. Working to raise the technological skills of young women is not the issue,' he shook his head, 'she has been doing this for many years.' Patience seized the opportunity to tap into what he said.

'Deputy, sir, with due respect, can you elaborate on what your thoughts are on this, please, so that I may comment if I can, on the matter.'

Patience embraced culture and values like a second skin. The male order had to be respected, first, if she hoped to gain more knowledge on the situation.

'Her brother, Biddhu, came to see her after all this time, this is no coincidence, you know. He was a poor man, barely able to feed his children – something there is eluding us.'

Patience disliked his circuitous way of dropping a few crumbs and then leaving her to guess what else he was thinking.

'Both were murdered, so please tell me, how did you arrive at that conclusion?' She had pushed the boundary and was unsure how much more he would reveal.

'Let's take a walk outside, sister. It's a bit too warm in here.'

Deputy Inspector Manik Lal was uncomfortable with Deepak within earshot, and his officers' inquisitive ears at the ever-ready. He hurried Patience out the door. They stood on the verandah. She whispered to Hiyana to stay in the schoolroom or kitchen, she was not going to leave her at the mercy of the roving eyes of the younger police officers.

'Sister Akanya Das returned from some training overseas, well that is what her assistant, sister Ojala indicated. I have no idea what the training entailed, but can safely surmise that it ruffled some feathers,' his circular head shaking indicated how serious he was in searching for the reason behind the murders. 'We are just not sure, how deep her commitment was to whatever training she underwent, to warrant us going through with investigating it further.'

Patience opted for silence on his views that rang true to her own. She was in the tight grip of the Mission's protocol.

'What makes you say that with such conviction, Deputy Inspector, sir?'

'There's nothing else, but this connection to something unknown about her overseas activity might be the key.'

'Have you spoken to Biddhu's wife?'

'Yes, indeed, I have. She says he behaved in an odd manner in recent weeks, leaving her and the children, for days at a time with no explanations about what he was doing. She said he became subdued, something changed him. There too, I suspect some other influence entered his life.'

'So, she had no idea where he had gone, and what he did during his bouts of absence from the home.'

'Correct.'

This left Patience with nothing else to say. He tapped her with his unfinished speculations in the hope that she would become the gushing fountain he needed. His life had taught him that women needed a semblance of coercion to tell it all. What he did not know was that Patience could be a barricaded fortress when she chose to conceal something. Mama Varuna's and Elsie's daughter upheld that the spreading of untruths, and the flouting of loyalty was forbidden.

Before she quizzed Alexis and Xandria, she had to speak to

Ojala – her silence had to be broken first. She invited her for a walk down Contemplation Lane.

Ojala was restless, worry etched in her cagey, searching eyes. 'What is it, sister Patience? Has something happened? Hiyana says you spoke to Inspector saab.'

'Nothing new, Ojala, but I am appealing to you to recall everything Akanya said to you about Biddhu's visit.'

Ojala looked away, heat coursed through her veins. Her past made her closed, and secretive. She was a living example of the long-term effects of domestic violence. Akanya gave her a second chance at life.

'Please, Ojala, I need the truth, we must prepare for the last rites ceremony, and as the priest indicated Akanya's soul will not be at rest if the rites are not performed.

Ojala was perturbed by that reminder.

'I do not want Kanya-ma to struggle in death too. All I know is that Biddhu came to see her and she seemed happy. The day before she disappeared, she said someone had been threatening to kill his family and she... she... felt she might have something to do with it.'

Ojala chose to keep this significant piece of information from the police for some strange reason.

'Is that it, did she say why she thought she might have something to do with the threat leveled at his family? Why did you choose to remain silent about an important piece of information?'

Ojala trembled like one found guilty for a crime she had committed.

'The people threatening him told him there would never be another female Prime Minister in this country. I could not say anything. Kanya-ma said we should never speak about her work, to anyone.'

The puzzle began to unfold, the judge's and Deputy Inspector Malik Lal's speculations became clear. The Mission's agenda for a

New World Order had fierce opposition in India. A vendetta against the organisation was a gruesome reality.

'Thank you, Ojala. That has been very helpful. If you recall anything else, please let me know.'

Patience had to talk to Alexis and Xandria before she spoke to the Deputy Inspector again.

Both refused to speak on the matter, leaving her furious.

She marched off to her room, shut the door and rang Masuyo.

'Hello Patience, Truth, Understanding and Compassion, this is a surprise, is everything going to plan?' Masuyo sounded hesitant, not her usual confident self.

'Far from it, I need answers, as Xandria and Alexis are sealed vaults, and that does not help me finish what I was sent here to do. Are you aware that Akanya might have been targeted and killed for her Mission involvement?'

Masuyo was quick to react.

'We are all victims when we engage in removing gender inequity.'

Patience felt swelling irritation. Why was Masuyo still adopting a politician's circuitous response when cornered?

'Please stop beating around the bush, tell me what to expect while you are safely in New York.' There, she said what had bothered her from the outset when she received the news of Akanya's situation. She was well and truly over this covert attitude. Masuyo had no option, she had to reveal that she had received an unsigned letter from India, telling her to stop her Mission activities in the region if she cared about the safety of the people who served her.

How far would Masuyo go to protect the Mission?

13

DILEMMA IN SPAIN

In the taxi en route to the hospital to see the dying mother of his child, both of whom were strangers to him, Keefe's brow moistened, his palms twitched, and his shirt collar tightened around his neck. He had no clue how he should begin a conversation with a woman he had met fleetingly during one drunken night in a pub, here in Spain, almost five years earlier. Guilt was second nature to him, he felt mam's look of chastisement all around him.

Trying to convince himself that he was ignorant to Carlos' existence, did nothing to stop him feeling like a criminal who deserved some sort of reckoning for his irresponsible behaviour. After many years of turning his back on religion, he shut his eyes and mentally summoned the saints he remembered, to guide him.

He paused at the door, made the sign of the cross and walked into the private ward to find Camila asleep. He peered at her face with no recollection. Illness had clearly ravaged her, no hint of familiarity surfaced, she remained a stranger.

After five minutes she wriggled and opened her eyes, turning to look at him. She rubbed her eyes and slowly pulled herself up on the bed.

'Keefe Daly?' she asked with no recollection in her searching eyes.

'Yes, Camila? How are you?' He felt like an idiot the second he asked such a thoughtless question when he had confirmation that she was dying – the very reason he was called to Spain.

'I've been better, but this is my life now, in and out of hospital until the final hour, I suppose. Don't feel awkward or sorry for me, I have come to terms with it.'

She put him at ease right away, understanding the shock he might have experienced at finding out he was a father, and might soon be the only living parent to Carlos. He suspected that she had rehearsed her little speech to avoid messing up their meeting.

'Thank you for doing the test, and coming all this way,' she added, 'it says to me that you are a good person, if you did not run away from what my attorney presented to you.' She stopped.

Keefe saw her struggle – her bluish lips, sparse hair, and unhealthy, deathly grey skin told the story of a once strong woman decimated by illness. Her nobility was in ensuring her son, their son, was her priority. He had to do the right thing for all the years she struggled to raise Carlos on her own, never once contacting him for financial support.

'I thought we should talk first before, Diane, my friend, brings Carlos in to see you, I fell asleep, watching the clock, waiting for you to arrive. I am just as nervous as you are.' She stopped, she tired quickly.

'Thank you for letting me know I had... we... had a child, and I am sorry for not knowing sooner...' He was awkward with what he wanted to say, and afraid he would be misinterpreted.

'No, it's meant to be this way. One night, not even one night, a couple of hours... I am ashamed to say... but I'm not going to make you marry me or send you on a guilt trip because I am equally to blame for what happened.'

'Let's leave that aside and look to what is best for Carlos, and what makes you happy and comfortable to accept.'

She smiled, 'Thank you.'

'Things are not as simple as I would like it to be. My partner is not happy that I want you to have custody of Carlos. That is your right, as his biological father.'

Keefe was silent on that revelation. He did not foresee opposition from a partner, or any other person associated with Camila. He shuddered with the realisation that her partner was the father Carlos knew, and perhaps loved. Where would that leave him? It was not right to ask why she chose him over her partner. Fear crept in. Perhaps he was not an ideal person to be the boy's father or carer? Then, she spoke as if she had read his thoughts.

'I was an adopted child. My mother gave me away because she was too young to be a single parent.' She stared at the ceiling for a few seconds, then continued, 'My parents were wonderful people, and I would not change that for anything in the world. I wanted... I spent my...' She reached for a drink of water, caught her breath and continued, 'I spent my entire teenage life and some of my adult life resenting the biological mother who threw me away. It filled me with self-loathing that my own mother did this to me, her child.'

Keefe listened, silent, grateful for the love mam had given him and Aileen.

'I never want Carlos to ever feel like that. He must know you, and if he chooses, when he is older, that you are not the father he wants, then it's up to him. Now, he needs to know you.'

He was stung by another pang of guilt that his first thought, when he received the letter requesting a DNA test, was that it could be a set-up, that somebody wanted to extort money from him.

'Thank you... if your wish is granted, I am definitely willing to raise Carlos...' He said it, confirmed it. He gave her his verbal promise. Her face lit up, and she reached out to touch his arm.

'Thank you, that's all I need to know. Diane will be here soon. You can have a ten-minute visit with Carlos today. You are a stranger to him, so please forgive him if he is shy or unfriendly, at first.'

As much as she wanted him to take custody of Carlos after her death, she had to be careful that Carlos was not alone with Keefe. He had to prove himself capable of engaging with the child before she let him have time alone with the boy.

'When you meet, Antonio, my partner, at some point, please be warned that he is a little hot-headed, so I apologise in advance. Our relationship has become strained after my decision to hand custody to you.'

Keefe felt another boulder rolling in his direction with a steep incline ahead of him. He had to brace himself for conflict. He wished Grace was there with her pragmatic advice.

Camila Flores was a matter-of-fact woman, a mother who wanted the best for her child. She wanted nothing else. The layers left unsaid about Antonio perturbed Keefe the most.

DIANE ARRIVED FIFTEEN MINUTES LATER. Clutching her legs and peering from behind her was a pair of penetrating blue eyes, shy and curious, looking up at his father. Keefe's pulse quickened. He had the overwhelming feeling of wanting to scoop the child up in his arms, hold him close and tell him everything was going to be just fine.

Camila's gentle voice broke through the moment.

'Tesoro, you look so handsome today, come give your momia a big kiss.'

Diane lifted Carlos who reached out to plant a wet kiss on his mother's cheek. She longed to hug him – the drip attached to her right arm and the burning, piercing sensation made it impossible. Carlos encircled her neck, with his little arms, in a gentle embrace.

'Mmmm, you smell nice, look at your beautiful hair.' She tried to raise her left arm to tousle his curly mop of red hair and withdrew when pain shot through her left side, down to her feet, leaving her breathless.

'Carlos, this is Keefe, your papi, corazón Don't be shy, give him a hug.' She nodded and smiled in encouragement. She had been preparing him for this moment.

Carlos put his finger in his mouth, and clung to Diane, whispering, 'No, no, no...'

He looked at Camila and said, 'Antonio, momia?'

Camila saw Keefe tense. 'Later, Carlos, you'll see Antonio later.' She looked at Keefe, 'Give him some time, he is a loving boy. He needs a little time.'

All Keefe heard in those words was her plea and determination to make her decision work. Her son will be with his father.

'He speaks a little English, so you will be able to talk to him. He's improving every day with Diane helping him. Give it a try,' she encouraged.

Keefe held out his hand to Carlos, inviting him to come closer. He walked up to his father with his finger still in his mouth. Keefe pulled him onto his lap. Camila smiled, quietly looking on.

Diane excused herself, to get a coffee. She gave them the privacy that was necessary for this first meeting.

Keefe pulled Carlos closer to his chest. The child relaxed and leaned back against him. The moment was nothing like Keefe had ever felt. A warmth encased him, he was bursting, he had to keep calm and gentle to win his son over, to allow a bond to form without rushing it. He stroked the child's head, saying nothing for a few seconds.

Then he whispered in Carlos' ear, 'I have something for you.'

He reached into his coat pocket and pulled out a little teddy-bear that fitted in the palm of his hand. Carlos smiled for the first time, took the little bear from him and rubbed it against his cheek. Keefe was grateful for Grace's advice to take something small to encourage a connection with the child.

Camila was quick to say, 'Say thank you to papi, Carlos.'

Carlos looked at Keefe with a smile, 'Thank you papi, I like it.'

He swallowed tears of joy. He held Carlos close to him, to fill his need to protect and love the boy.

Footsteps hurried outside on the corridor and the door burst open. Carlos jumped off Keefe's lap, calling out in joy, 'Antonio, Antonio!' The dark-haired, athletic figure swept the child into his arms, holding him tight as he glared across at Keefe.

Camila's agitation was obvious, her face was flushed as she tried to lift herself higher up on the narrow bed. She sucked in her breath when she felt the searing burn from the drip.

'Antonio! You are not supposed to be here.' She raised her voice, mustering the strength to chastise him.

'Nothing will keep me away from stopping OUR son being taken by this stranger!' His voice was too loud in a high-care facility.

The nurse on duty rushed in.

Keefe was astounded when Camila said, 'Please remove this man, he is not supposed to be here. He's distressing me.'

Keefe felt faint, firstly from the exhaustion of the flight, then the emotional connection to Carlos, and now this intrusion on his first visit to meet his son. The nurse told Antonio to leave as he was distressing the patient, or she would ring security to have him removed. What had started out with good intention, took an unexpected turn, leaving Keefe wondering if he had done the right thing by coming to Spain.

BACK AT HIS HOTEL ROOM, he called Grace.

It was 7:30 am in Australia, Grace would be home after her shift handover.

'Good morning, mo ghrá, how are you? Did you have a good night at work?'

'Keefe! It's good to hear your voice. I'm well thanks and had a good, slow night at ER. Have you met little Carlos yet?'

'Long story. Make yourself a coffee, I'll call you back in fifteen minutes, if that's okay with you.'

'Now you have me worried. I will call you back since you are at the hotel. I'll get that coffee, like the good doctor ordered,' she laughed nervously with rising dread.

Sobered by her first morning shot of coffee, she returned Keefe's call. She listened to his recount of seeing Camila and Carlos, and Antonio's rude intrusion.

'Was he aggressive?'

'More emotional that a stranger was coming to take the child. I have not legally agreed to anything yet, it must be Camila telling him my intention.'

'Interesting that she hasn't opted to give him custody of the child. Perhaps he is irresponsible as displayed in your first encounter with him.'

'Who knows what to think, at this stage. I'm seeing the attorney that ordered the DNA test in the morning. Hopefully this will give me a neutral view into how to proceed, now that there is a challenge, to the smooth run I expected.'

Grace loved listening to the warmth in Keefe's voice when he spoke of Carlos as 'mini-me.' He accepted that it was his responsibility to step in while Camila was ill, and if needed, take full control of his care.

At ten o' clock the next morning, a freshly shaven, suited Keefe, with a well-pressed crisp shirt, waited in the foyer of *Flores and Sons,* Attorneys at Law since 1902 – an established family business that bore Camila's last name had him a little curious to know if they were related.

A short, stout man, greying at the temples stepped out from behind the receptionist.

'Keefe Daly?' He stood up and walked through the door to the right of the foyer.

Keefe extended his hand, 'Nice to meet you, Mr Flores.'

A firm handshake followed by, 'Matteo, please. Good to meet you Keefe.' His appreciative glance at Keefe's presentability confirmed that he had gained the first green tick of approval.

After the offer of a cup of coffee, a brief chat on the weather and opinions on the Australian Open Tennis Tournament, Matteo got down to business.

'I'm sorry that Antonio caused a disturbance at the hospital. From what I've been told, he has been erratic ever since Camila's diagnosis. He is struggling with all of this.'

'He must love her very much, but I need to know what I am up against. It's clear that I'm perceived as the enemy.'

'Si, it's an emotional reaction, he is a hot-headed man, Italian,' he laughed.

Keefe did not appreciate the dismissive reaction to his question and wondered whether the attorney was partial to Antonio for other reasons. 'Are you Camila's relative? Your surname suggests you might be related.'

'A distant cousin, Camila felt she had to have someone she could trust to represent her. Her intention is to give Carlos the best opportunity in life. It's all legal, if that's what you are concerned about, Dr Daly.' The sudden formality from the first relaxed introduction, made Keefe uncomfortable.

Matteo Flores seemed honest enough. All he cared about was that the legal side of Carlos' care was in place. He made it clear that Camila intended for Keefe to take full custody of Carlos.

Paperwork had to be completed, bonding with Carlos was essential and all he had, was a week to achieve this or he would have to return to Spain.

Matteo made it seem like there was no problem and chose not

to discuss the upheaval Antonio could create or whether he had any legal right to contest Camila's decision.

Keefe had to ask the question that vexed him the most.

'What if Antonio attempts to take the child?'

'As in an abduction? I don't think he will do that, but if it's worrying you, I will order surveillance around Antonio to ensure that does not happen.'

Keefe's gut told him that Antonio was going to rock the boat and spin him around in the hope that he would give up and return to Australia.

14

TWO FUNERALS

The investigation in Panna pointed to a vendetta against the Mission for a New World Order. Masuyo arranged for Alexis and Xandria to return to New York as soon as possible after Akanya's cremation.

A covert counter movement had begun in India and had been operating for the past six months ever since they got wind of the Mission's objectives. While the media covered the story of three recruits, more information had leaked from inside the Mission. Trust and truth were compromised – all agents in India were in danger.

Akbar arrived from Pakistan. He was delighted to see Patience again, but equally saddened and disturbed by the situation at hand with Akanya's murder. His fatherly advice at their first meeting was to proceed with caution, noting any strangers who could not be accounted for at the centre.

'In effect we are all strangers to each other as it stands.' Patience accepted his warning and let him proceed with no questions asked.

'Yes, even more reason anyone whose identity is not known as in who they are, why they are here, and who they represent must be sought and treated with suspicion. The time and situation decree this, so forget being hospitable if the individual is unknown to us.'

Akbar appreciated Patience's warm, and hospitable nature but felt the urgency to spell out the dire need to proceed with utmost care with newcomers. She was after all a foreigner in this region, ignorant to the extent of the vendetta.

He scheduled a meeting with Deputy Inspector Manik Lal to finalise the security measures for the day of the funeral. The retired judge in Bangalore provided startling facts on Biddhu's activities. He was on the payroll of the Anti-Mission League, a band of a hundred-and-fifty rebels billeted around India to snuff out any moves to establish a female head of state.

Akanya was safe in the years during which she ran the IT centre for dislocated, forgotten women in Panna. She gained attention after her involvement with the Mission. Patience squirmed at the pride that came with being head-hunted by an international organisation – now being a member held a death sentence. To her, this made the Mission culpable in Akanya's murder. She was sick to the stomach when evidence suggested that Biddhu led the murderers to his sister. He sacrificed his sister for money and the promise of a lavish lifestyle. She pondered whether Akanya was aware that the half-brother she was elated to be reunited with, was in over his head in rebel activities. Poverty drove people to do desperate things to survive, but honest, caring Akanya never questioned why her brother reappeared in her life. Being alone in the world, with no next of kin, was as awful as living a life of poverty.

Akanya had Ojala's, the Panna Centre's and her students' love and respect, but her yearning for her biological family ran deep. Her mother's life of loneliness as a single parent, and as a victim of patriarchal abuse, stole her capacity to raise her daughters in the best way she could – this instilled a longing for family. She lived by her version of the adage, 'Blood is thicker than water,' but also added that when blood runs thin, as she had often seen, she drank the untainted water around her. Patience enjoyed listening to Akanya's philosophical nuggets of wisdom.

With gentle persuasion, Akbar gained more information from Manik Lal, he sang like a nightingale. He had a captive audience in Akbar who soaked up every drop of information he shared. He agreed to place police officers on watch – two at the funeral, one at the centre's main entrance and two at the crematorium.

Patience scoffed at what good the police would do to protect them. The only decent policeman among them was Manik Lal. The others were narcissistic perverts with an appetite for power. In a place where lawlessness pervaded, it seemed the police became more corrupt than the criminals. They brushed aside the seriousness of Akanya's murder until Manik Lal made his voice heard to prevent this becoming a cold case.

The priest who was to preside over the last rites arrived at the centre to discuss the arrangements with Ojala. She asked for Patience to be present as a backup to ensure she understood the list of requirements.

'Finally, we are ready to put sister to rest. Tch, tch, tch, too, too long.' He wagged his bulbous finger at Ojala who cowered in silence, afraid to speak. He turned to Patience, smiled and explained why time was significant to ensure a peaceful departure after death.

'Sister Akanya was murdered, an unnatural end to life. Her soul's disturbed by this act of violence against her. When we delay in purifying her path across from the living plane to the nether plane, we leave her soul wandering, like a lost, frightened child.' His hands and head complemented the passionate belief he held in the unnaturalness of untimely death, and delays in performing the last rites. 'This in turn adds to the stress of the universe in the negative energy it creates, in the mind and soul of grieving families, in this case colleagues and students. All this has an impact on global peace, you see.' He looked at Patience for acknowledgement.

She was fascinated by his explanation of the significance of the last ritual.

'I will provide a chant that all the householders here, *must* engage in, at dawn and dusk, leading up to Friday. This chant will soothe our dear sister's distressed soul. Keep the lamps burning night and day, infuse the surroundings with incense. This will light her path to the other side.' As he dished out each instruction, he raised his arms heavenwards with a quick sideward glance for Patience's reaction.

At first, she thought him to be an impatient man. Now in sharing his wisdom on life and death, she appreciated why he hurried to conclude things.

'It makes sense, thank you, sir.' Patience bowed in reverence.

'No, not sir, guruji is enough. I am no grand sire, just a humble servant of our Great Lord. You, sister, have much to teach the world on tolerance and compassion.'

'Thank you, you are too kind, guruji.'

His head bobbed with pride and joy to see one so open to understanding why the scriptures set out birth and death as it did. The thing that bemused her was his genial attitude to her and irritation when Hiyana and Ojala asked a question. His gender bias had a distinct national border restriction! She enjoyed his wisdom but was annoyed by his double standards.

Later when she spoke of his reverence and humility in not wanting to be called 'sir' but 'guruji' instead, Hiyana sneered, 'That's a pretence of humility, 'guruji' is his claim to be respected as the grand teacher. Where's the humility in that!'

The gender divide had deep roots, that someone as young as Hiyana could speak with a vengeful old head on cultural truths.

Akbar took a stroll on Contemplation Lane with Patience after the priest left.

'Sister Patience, please let me know how I can help with the arrangements for Friday, anything at all. I am aware, like back home, that men discredit whatever a woman requests, well in most cases. I should add, there are some good men, doing the right thing without gender discrimination. Did everything go as expected with the priest?'

Thank you, yes brother, it did. You are a godsend with the challenges faced here. I imagine that was Masuyo's foresight in requesting that you come over.'

'Yes, she has her strategies which I respect, but we have to move things along here. We must return to our posts without delay after Friday. Duty calls at home.'

Patience told him about the chanting request in the days leading up to Akanya's cremation.

'We can all do this, whatever it takes to send sister off in peace. When do we begin? I can do my sunrise and evening prayer at the same time.'

Akbar's ability to embrace all in acceptance of what faith meant to each was admirable. Masuyo chose him as her second in charge of the Mission in the East. He was a mover and shaker with values that spoke out in favour of women for unified world peace.

Patience recalled that Akanya, as a humble being, shared a secret desire to be a Bollywood actress and laughed it off as a wild thought. Today the Mission ensured it spared no expense in sending off one of its own in grand style. Flowers arrived in abundance. Bags of rice, potatoes, and boxes of pristine vegetables in preparation for a grand farewell.

Ojala asked if Biddhu would be farewelled with Akanya. Patience and Ming had grave reservations and thought it best to contact his wife. She declined, saying she wanted a private funeral for the husband she had lost many months before his death. With no next of kin to protest, it was set that Akanya would be cremated and her ashes buried beside her mother and sister.

During the days in the week of Akanya's funeral, everybody

wore flowing robes, the kimonos Masuyo sent to India, for use during the chanting sessions to prepare the path for release as the priest had instructed. The lamp glowed with an unwavering light, continuously burning, day and night. Deepak and Hiyana were vigilant that it remained lit. During these days calm fell over the centre. Deepak sounded a gentle gong as a reminder for the gathering in the dining hall. It was the largest space at the centre. Mats were rolled out and everybody sat cross-legged on the floor as Hiyana led the morning and evening chant in her soft, melodious voice.

The silent and often unseen Alexis and Xandria prepared the farewell speech on behalf of the Mission. Patience marveled at how their roles had changed from the days at the mysterious training camp, to Panna, at Akanya's centre. They chose obscurity either from fear of detection by counter forces, or they were instructed to remain aloof. The Mission was still very much a secret operation. Trainers were out in the world while Masuyo was at HQ preparing for the next round of training. Akanya's death had forced her to rethink how she would expedite the next training session without placing the new recruits at risk. The role of women and political thought, it could not be denied, were still within a patriarchal grip. The Mission was a necessary agency for change that could not be deterred by opposition.

A large marquee erected in the grounds of the centre, filled the tight space on a narrow, long property. A large screen at the front and two smaller screens on the sides beamed with the smiling face of Akanya Das with her large black dot, dead centre on her forehead. Some of her endearing advice scrolled beneath her image. For the first time Patience noted the soft, distant look in her eyes – the eyes of pain and suffering that looked beyond the immediate, searching with child-like curiosity. The eyes of a humble being, with a spirit so large that she affected all who surrounded her. Her presence vibrated in the space. Everybody walked in with clasped palms in acknowledgement of the departed soul. Large vases with fresh white roses and one single red rose among them were placed on concrete stands to decorate the interior periphery. The air was perfumed with the exotic combination of flowers and incense.

Ming sat next to Patience with her head bowed. Throughout their days at the Panna Centre, she had little to say. Now an endless flood of tears rushed down her face. She had insulated herself before the funeral, Patience accepted it was best to let her work through her tide of emotions in meditative quietness. But, something more than Akanya's death had shaken Ming's equilibrium.

During Alexis' farewell speech, a disturbance at the entrance of the marquee, down at the far end, annoyed mourners. A woman's voice protested being stopped by a police officer. She explained that she was a close associate of Akanya Das. Patience recognised the voice and walked up to the entrance to meet a red-faced Audra.

'They won't let me in. I'm family. Tell them, Patience.'

Patience escorted her to the front row. Audra whispered, 'Thank god, I made it on time. I would not have forgiven myself if I missed Akanya's funeral. Poor soul!'

Xandria read out a few messages from Mission members that she referred to as close 'friends' of Akanya.

After the formalities, the priest led the coffin out for the trek to the crematorium. A dignified group of mourners followed behind the coffin, chanting in lowered voices as Akanya made her final trip to her resting place. Patience, Ming, Audra, Alexis and Xandria walked side-by-side, with Akbar behind them. The Mission, a united front, walked the last sombre journey with their chosen one.

The silence was broken when Hiyana lifted her fist and belted out, 'Kanya-ma,' 'Kanya-ma', 'Kanya-ma' – some did the same in a celebratory outpour of respect. Akbar tapped Patience on the shoulder, 'Amazing! The spirit of these women is amazing!' He

lifted his fist up and followed Hiyana's open, youthful demonstration of love. Soon every person following the procession to the
crematorium did the same. It was only then that Patience noticed
a television crew rushing to the front of the crowd to get footage
of Hiyana. She feared what this would mean for Hiyana once her
face hit the headlines.

That night all the householders at the Panna Centre gathered
in the dining hall to draw strength from each other. It hit home,
that Akanya was gone but her legacy was alive and in need of a
new leader.

Hiyana and Ojala spoke of what they remembered as their
special personal interactions with Akanya. They asked Patience
for her favourite recollection. She stood up, 'It would have to be
her mothering way, and her elaborate hand gestures, which I
think would have made her a great mime artist!' Everybody
laughed, nodding in agreement, 'but, I loved her generous,
forgiving nature, the most.'

Patience caught a glimpse of Deputy Inspector Manik Lal, he
sat next to Audra who called out, 'I second that! We all loved that
about her.' He nodded in acknowledgement of catching
Patience's eye. Audra asked if she could spend a night at the
centre. The organisation had mastered fostering allegiance
amongst its members, it was alive and vibrant as Akanya was laid
to rest. Patience retired, ready to collapse in a heap when she
received a text message from Grace. She started writing a long
reply when her phone rang.

'Sorry to call you so late, I had to speak to you. How are you?
Did everything go to plan with the funeral?' The anxiety in
Grace's rushed questions was obvious.

'Thankfully it did. I am exhausted but happy that Akanya had
a grand send-off. How are things on the home front? Any further
news from Keefe?'

'We can chat about Keefe another time. The reason I had to

call you now, is that Alf has passed away. I know nothing else at this stage. He died earlier today.'

Patience felt a heavy weight collapse on her. Alf was dead, and here she was, all the way in India, having barely laid a dear colleague to rest. Felicity would need her now, more than ever...

15

AIRPORT DRAMA

Antonio complicated Keefe's final signing of the custody documents. He lodged a counter claim to the effect that he deserved the right to be the only father Carlos had and needed. He cited his emotional connection, and the detrimental impact separation would have for the boy in losing his mother, and the father he knew. To add to his case, he presented unfounded evidence that Camila was not of sound mind in deciding that Keefe should have custody of Carlos.

Keefe arrived in Sydney, dejected and lost as he sauntered to passport control. The automatic passport check was not working, queues of exhausted travellers waited in frustration. The woman attending to Keefe, scrutinised his passport and told him to step aside. Two police officers approached and asked him to follow them for questioning. Keefe was emotionally drained, and anger surfaced.

'What is this about? I'm not a criminal and I'm not carrying dangerous goods. You have made a mistake.'

'You are Keefe Daly. We have a few questions, please bear with us.'

'Questions? On what?'

'You are an Irish citizen, a recent Australian resident currently working as a doctor.'

'Yes, my passport clearly states that.'

'You were in Spain this past week. What was the nature of your business there?'

Keefe shut his eyes in disbelief, this must be a dream, he thought, why was this happening?

'I traveled there to meet my son, for the first time. His mother is dying and requested I come over.'

'Were you requested to go for a visit, only?'

'The mother of the child wants me to have custody of our son, her health is deteriorating rapidly, and she wants to ensure the boy does not end up in foster care. May I leave now?'

The officer posing the questions, stiffened.

'Were you subjected to a DNA test to prove paternity? Answer yes or no, only.'

'Yes.'

'Did you deny you were the father that a test had to be ordered?'

Keefe's body prickled with rage at the insinuation that he was irresponsible.

'I did not know of his birth until the test was ordered. You have not told me why you are investigating my trip to Spain.'

He hated this intrusion into his private life. Irritation was likely to make him say something he would regret for the rest of his life. A cautionary voice in his head told him to comply with the questions, prove that he is who he says he is, and that he had no criminal intentions, if that's what they were after.

'Did you have intent to take the child without completing the required legal process in Spain?'

The picture cleared with that question. He was a victim of a vendetta that wanted to stop him being Carlos' legal guardian – Antonio had had his way across international borders!

'May I make a call please, to my partner, I do believe, with that question, I need legal back-up.'

'A lawyer is not necessary, at this stage. You may make your telephone call.'

The officer looked at Keefe as a man who did not appear to be deviant. He had encountered the best in society who sometimes performed the most atrocious crimes, in their desire to fill their emotional needs.

Grace arrived forty minutes later. She called Felicity for a quick legal look at what had happened to Keefe. She hated disturbing her during her period of mourning. The advice she received was that no legal recourse was necessary. It appeared to be a check from a tip-off.

'I can verify why my partner had to go to Spain and I can also provide you with telephone numbers to call a few people to confirm if Keefe is lying or telling the truth. This is a most ridiculous situation. There are real crimes out there, why waste taxpayer's money chasing what is not a crime or illegal in any way!'

Keefe wished Grace would stop. She was annoyed and would have a say when she saw hypocrisy.

'That won't be necessary madam. Dr Daly is free to leave.'

Keefe questioned for the third time why he was hauled in for this line of questioning like some border patrol incident seen on television.

'We apologise for the inconvenience. With the new terror laws...'

Keefe flew off the handle, before the officer could complete his sentence.

'I don't believe this! So, is everybody a suspected terrorist when pulled out for questioning?'

Grace touched Keefe's arm and urged him to let the officer finish what he was saying.

'Not at all, we do not consider you a terrorist. We received a message from Spain after your flight departed that an anonymous caller named you as a child abductor and paedophile. This was serious enough to investigate to prove whether it was a hoax or legitimate.'

'Absurd! I am trying to do the right thing. If I am guilty of anything, it is not knowing I had a child in Spain. The mother chose not to divulge this until now. I've said enough already. I do believe I know who the anonymous caller is, tell your Spanish connection he's the one to watch!'

'We apologise once again. We are under orders to investigate all reports received given the current political and social climate.'

Two scarlet faced police officers watched them walk away.

Keefe had time to simmer down on the drive home.

'This has got to be the worst time in my life. What should have been a significant time in my life, has turned sour. Who knows with all this going on whether Camila will be able to fulfil her dying wish? Antonio, has a lot to answer, I will have to think through how to respond.'

Grace felt the beginning of their problems burning on the horizon. She hoped for both their sakes that Carlos would be reunited with Keefe. Having him close was the only option he would accept. Now that he discerned that his child was in danger of being snatched from him, by his mother's irate partner, his determination grew.

'Are you going to let Camila know what happened today?'

'I suppose I should, although she has much to deal with after Antonio claimed she is not of sound mind.'

They decided not to talk any further on the matter that day to allow themselves the joy of being with each other.

FELICITY WANTED a private funeral for Alf, Grace and Keefe would attend if Patience was not back from India. Felicity and Alf had an elaborate wedding, state of the art everything, now she opted for simplicity. She was done with the fanfare of life. Grace called to update Felicity on the airport travesty before she slipped out for her shift that evening, leaving Keefe in a deep sleep.

Andrew was anxious and wanted to know more after he received Grace's text message about the airport situation.

'It really upsets me how criminals get away – rapists are set free, paedophiles are released and what happens? They go right back to their old dirty ways! Yet an innocent man can be made to feel like a criminal!'

'Poor Keefe, it was a horrid experience. By the way did the police call you to ask if you knew why Keefe went to Spain?'

'No... why would they?'

'I gave them your name, Felicity's and Patience's details if they wanted to verify why Keefe was in Spain. Being his partner, I thought they would surmise that I was complicit in whatever he was supposedly doing.'

Grace had had enough of a testosterone driven world for one day.

'It has all been a bit much, overreactions if you ask me. The source of the call should have been investigated. I daresay it's changing times that bring strange happenings.'

'True, let's get to it Dr Sharvin after we've had some coffee to fire the brain and fuel the blood!'

Grace laughed when she heard her words in Andrew's authoritarian voice.

'It's good that you're laughing again. We need some joy after this endless accumulation of morose news.'

Andrew left the building to source coffee from a new coffee house on the street. Hospital regulation coffee had lost its effect on them.

Beth Hobbs arrived early on shift allowing Grace time to make a call to Patience.

'Hey, this is a surprise aren't you at work tonight?'

'I am, but Beth is holding the fort, so I decided to call you, for a quick chat while it's quiet in here.'

'Good, any news from Felicity? How is she doing?'

'Yeah, I spoke to her but on a different matter. Don't think me insensitive, but I will have more news on Alf's funeral soon. You know Felicity, its business as usual for her. She wants to have a private funeral, but the date has not been announced yet.'

'I hope to be back home in time to attend Alf's funeral. What matter did you have to speak to Felicity about? Is there a problem?'

Patience always sensed a problem when her sister called, with no forewarned text message, to hear her voice with supposedly nothing much to report.

'It will be great to have you back home. Nothing much, I'll tell you all when you get back.'

Grace had no intention of weighing Patience down with her news on Keefe's latest fiasco.

'Forgive my poor memory, is Keefe back from Spain?'

'He sure is. He might have to return, soon, to finalise the paperwork for his custody rights. One week was too short a time to get it all done.'

'Oh dear, he has a lot on his plate. How much time does the mother have?'

'Not a lot, I'm afraid, by the look of things. But a mother's love will keep her hanging on until she settles her little boy.'

'I hope so, Gracie. On my front Masuyo has asked me to check in on Ojala to estimate whether she will cope with running the Panna Centre.'

Grace paused, confused by the implication of what Patience was asked to do.

'I thought Akanya ran her own ship, that she was the sole leader of the centre she set up. Why is Masuyo controlling what happens there?'

With all the emotional and political turbulence leading up to the cremation, Patience missed this obvious fact.

'You are absolutely right, I never gave it a thought. I will check on this. Thank you, good thinking 99!'

She left her with a new dilemma.

Patience appeared to have accepted being a pawn to the Mission's whims. What had happened to her feisty little sister who questioned everything?

Andrew returned with three large coffees, mindful to include Beth Hobbs.

'What's that in the bag? Cake?'

'A mango cheesecake just what the doctor ordered.' Andrew smiled with his usual full-toothed, boyish grin.

'You are incorrigible, who eats cheesecake on the nightshift in an ER facility?'

'We do now, and there's enough to take home a slice for Keefe in the morning'

'Dr Lang, I ought to fire you!' Grace laughed.

They cast off the angst of the day as they prepared to mend those who struggled that night. She watched Andrew leave her office – her secret wish had been for Andrew and Virginia to be a couple, but this was not meant to be.

The evening quietened down around midnight. Grace checked her emails. A name loomed in her inbox. 'Anton Wessels.' She had not thought of him nor had she spoken of him in years. She opened her email and read:

Dear Grace,

This must come as a surprise hearing from me after all these years, hey! I will be in Sydney in a few months' time and would like to see you and Patience. I finally sold the woodyard that your dear mother so kindly left me when you all moved to Australia. Lots has happened, and I could not sustain running the yard, any longer. I will explain everything when I see you in a few months. I will be in touch to keep you informed of my arrival date. I have only recently discovered from someone who knows your family, that madam, your mother, passed away. I am so sorry for your loss. Best wishes, Anton.

Grace read and reread the email, reeling from the shock that Anton had tracked her down on her work email address. She was guilty of not pursuing a bounced email to Anton on her mother's tragic death. It was thoughtless of her to leave him uninformed. Anton was an honest worker and loyal to her mother when family had cut them off after her father's death.

Memories of her father's woodyard flooded back on the pendulum of good times and the horror of her first encounter with Boetie Arendse. The sale of the woodyard marked the end of an era for her family. Her mother refused to sell the woodyard when they moved to Australia. She named Anton as the best person to run it and signed over ownership to him. She would not accept that Anton wanted to send her a percentage of the takings each month. For her, seeking a new life meant she should not carry the baggage of the past with her.

Her father had worked hard at the woodyard. At first it was a humble, small business and soon grew into a massive empire that courted family jealousy. He did the best he could to ensure she and Patience and their mothers had the comfort they deserved.

The past had returned while her father's murder remained unsolved.

16

THE PANNA CENTRE

Patience observed Ojala – her compassion and understanding were her primary traits – her social engagements were marked by her awkward, quiet and unapproachable disposition. Serving others was her strength, it allowed her to remain silent on the shame that was forced upon her. In her married life, the continuous put downs, the fists in her face, kicks, bleeding head and lips, left her afraid, and unsure of how to be herself. Patience believed that Ojala could recover her self-esteem, but she had a long way to go before she could lead the centre. The Mission fast-tracked women for leadership roles with intense training at off-site locations throughout the world. Perhaps this was the way for her. In the interim, the question of who was going to step into the role was a burden thrust upon Patience.

Grace's unsettling thought that the Mission's involvement with the Panna Centre had deeper connections left her antsy for the truth. It was hopeless asking Xandria and Alexis who were scheduled to fly back to New York that evening. They remained stoic, just as tight-lipped as they were during the Mission training days. Masuyo never withheld the truth, never overtly lying, and after much deliberation she would reveal the truth, only exposing what she thought appropriate to share, and then appealed for secrecy until she was ready for a public announcement.

She called Masuyo to outline her observations of Ojala's leadership skills and was surprised to discover that she was aware of Ojala's traumatised past. The Mission's access to personal information baffled her. This was how she had been head-hunted for leadership training. The challenges accrued when Masuyo declared that Ojala was not the right person to lead the centre. There was no opportunity to question whether the Panna Centre was a branch of the Mission.

Hiyana brought her a fresh towel and a warm cup of turmeric tea. She had the skills to head the centre, but she was too young, at eighteen, to assume full leadership. Masuyo would only sanction such a recommendation if an experienced woman guided her until she was ready for total immersion in the role.

Hiyana wrote beautiful poems and sang with the melodious voice of an angel. Her physical attributes, if known, would be netted by Bollywood and Hollywood film makers. Her perceptiveness and obvious intelligence grew from her voracious reading which made her an interesting conversationalist. She had so much to her advantage including being just and headstrong on women's issues. Patience invited Hiyana to spend the afternoon with her. She needed to tap into her goals to understand her vision for the future of women in her country.

'Tell me more about yourself. You are an intelligent young woman, how is that you are not doing any tertiary study?'

'I came here after both my parents were killed in a car crash, two years ago. My extended family, especially my father's brother, wanted me to marry one of his business associates. I left when I was aware of Kanya-ma's centre and have been here ever since. Kanya-ma has taught me so much on technology and how to be humble. I love it here! A fund was started for me to study at the Indian Institute of Technology – now with Kanya-ma's passing I'm not sure what will happen. I will apply for other scholarships, will you help with the applications, sister Patience?'

'Absolutely! I am thrilled that you are going to study further.' Her mind ticked with thoughts of Hiyana studying through the Open Universities in Australia, and that she had the freshness, talent and capacity, with additional guidance, to make a difference anywhere in the world.

They spent a pleasant afternoon writing poems and philosophising about the world now, and what they desired for the future.

Akbar was leaving for Pakistan in the morning. Patience hoped he had information on the Mission's involvement at the Panna Centre.

After dinner that evening when Alexis and Xandria had made their exit from India, Patience asked Akbar to join her for tea in the dining room. She told Deepak and Hiyana to take the night off after the hectic week at the centre.

Akbar was honest in his interactions with Patience, but she believed that some information from the Mission might be withheld from him. He had no idea why the Mission aborted her time at the Well Study Centre in Pakistan before her full three months was over. She got straight to the matter with him, and he respected her direct manner. He had the opportunity, during her months in Pakistan, to get to know her well. When her happy disposition waxed and waned, he understood that something troubled her.

'What has disturbed you, sister? You appear unhappy tonight.'

'The Mission has. If it's an off-limits topic, stop me.'

Never in his association with her had he heard this, abrupt cut to the chase attitude. She was direct, but never abrupt.

'The only time anything is off-limits, as you know, is when I don't have the knowledge to share, or I am under a directive to maintain a code of secrecy. Ask and I hope I have an answer for you.'

She looked at this wise man that she met almost a year ago. A man whose daughters could not have hoped for a better father. They formed a connection almost immediately, like two who had met in a previous life. Uniting in goals and values draws people from all walks of life together – language, race, culture or creed are insignificant when a common purpose is to uplift a brother or sister in need.

'Thank you, for your honesty. Is this centre a Mission centre? I was under the impression that it was Akanya's centre, that she established the women's technology school and residence.'

'You must have encountered some bureaucracy to ask this. Has Masuyo issued a directive?'

'Not a directive, per se, but she has asked for my opinion on whether Ojala could head this centre and then rejected the possibility.'

'I see. What I know is that this centre was initiated and set up by sister Akanya. Eighteen months ago, headquarters took control of running the centre to assist her. The centre was growing exponentially, and sister needed help. She approached the Mission because she could not find suitable, moral decision makers. Those who approached her wanted a hefty pay cheque.'

'Thank you, my sixth sense suggested as much. She has achieved so much here that it disturbed me to think that it might have been taken away from her.'

Silence, for a few seconds, marked their deep respect for the departed Akanya.

'It was sister's choice. We are neighbours yet we never met in the living years. What a great pity. I know of the amazing things she has done.'

'May she rest in blissful, eternal peace.'

Akbar placed his hand on his heart.

'It will not be the same around here, after you've left for

Pakistan. Ming heads back to China soon, she's been reclusive. It is her nature, but I think something is not right. I have to figure out how to approach her.'

Her ability to be in the moment with everyone, noticing what made them happy, sad or distressed is what Akbar hoped his daughters would develop in their interactions with others.

'People respond differently when grieving, some withdraw, others are overly demonstrative.'

'I guess so. Tell me about your family. How are your wife and daughters? Is Azmil well?'

'My daughters are ready to take up their tertiary studies now. They have chosen Australia as the place for them, I'm told.'

'Great! We have the best universities. If they decide on New South Wales, remember I can be the bridge in helping them settle in.'

'You are wonderful to offer that. I've left it to them to decide which university offer they will accept. My wife will remain in Pakistan and visit once they are settled.'

'You live the Mission's values by giving your daughters the best opportunity in life.'

'Values come from faith and upbringing which drew me to the Mission.'

She heard the value in his words and understood that this too, was her reason for being drawn to the Mission.

'Azmil is keen to visit Australia. He might accompany my daughters on the trip there. You might see him then.'

'Nothing will delight me more than to host them when they arrive in Australia.'

'Thank you, dear Patience. My daughters refer to you as 'Australian Aunty,' he smiled, 'so they've claimed you as family.'

'That makes me very happy.'

They parted as old friends, yet Akbar bowed in respect to her, placed his hand on his heart and wished her a pleasant night.

Hiyana checked in on Patience prior to settling for the night. She enjoyed the wisdom, honesty and humour they shared.

The whirring ceiling fan did nothing to cool the sultry night. The open windows failed to invite a breeze. Thoughts of Audra's dissatisfaction that Akanya was privileged during their training days sprung into Patience's overactive mind. Ming laughed off such a notion at the time – the truth had a way of seeping back – Audra was quick to pick up that Akanya's connection to the Mission went beyond that of a recruit.

Akbar confirmed her suspicion and that was all she needed to know. She called Felicity without sending a text message prior to her call as she always did. Felicity's no-frills advice was needed to ground her thinking. Even though Felicity was in mourning their bond allowed unplanned calls between them when the need arose.

'This is a surprise, Patience! How are you?'

'Forget about how I'm doing. How are you? I am so sorry for not calling sooner. My sincere condolences on Alf's passing, you were in my thoughts, but I cannot begin to explain the chaos here, hence my fleeting text messages to you. Alf is free from pain and suffering now, you must miss him, but God knows best.'

Silence on the other end of the line had her worried. Perhaps it was an inappropriate time to call.

Felicity's soft voice replied, 'Yeah, thank you, I miss him. But our number is called at some point, you know. Alf had a good innings, he prepared himself mentally to go and asked that I not waste time mourning as there's much to be done in the world.'

Felicity was Felicity, frank without considering the gravity of her words. Her subdued voice conveyed her sadness, but her brave respect in honouring Alf's wish made Patience feel a longing for such love. Mutual love and respect are fundamental to ensuring the longevity of such a memory. The denial of this need led so many women to her SHSO door.

'Yes, that is why we must make peace here on earth, fulfil our desires, and love like we've never loved.'

'What's this now?' Felicity laughed, 'being in India has been good for you. I detect a spiritual awakening!'

'I don't know about that. It has been a rollercoaster ride but being so close to Akanya's legacy has been humbling.'

'I look forward to hearing all about it, in person. When do you get back home?'

'I hope to make it for Alf's funeral, but things are still up in the air here on who will take over running the Panna Centre.'

'You have to do what you have to do. Please don't tell me you have been elected to run the place.'

'I should be there to support you. No, I won't be running the centre. I have lots to do at my SHSO.'

'That's good, at least I have hope of seeing you again!' Felicity explained that Alf requested a private funeral, he wanted no fuss. She slipped in Keefe's airport incident which came as a surprise – Grace had not uttered a word about it in their recent conversation. Felicity's revelation left a hollow feeling – why had Grace deliberately kept her in the dark on such an important family issue?

'Chances are Keefe might not get the child, after all that.'

This conversation created a wave of sadness that Patience was not expecting. She questioned why Grace chose to confide in Felicity of all people, on such a grave personal matter. Was she upset with her for some reason? They had a solid relationship that had weathered so much, why the secrecy now? Wild thoughts exhausted her, and a migraine took hold. Grace was thrilled that a child was moving in with them. She had started looking at houses, saying her apartment was not the ideal home to raise a child. Now with this awful news from Felicity, she feared that Grace might have slipped into a bout of depression. Things had to be bleak if she chose to speak to Felicity on the matter. This was a change she had not anticipated. Anxiety and disappointment exacerbated her migraine.

17

MY SON, MY CHILD

In the early hours of Friday morning, Keefe received news from Camila's attorney.

Keefe. Sorry to be the bearer of sad news. Camilla passed away at 5:30 this afternoon. I will be in touch.

Keefe jumped out of bed, walked across to the couch, his head abuzz with how lost and afraid little Carlos would be without his mother. Did he understand what death meant? Had Camila prepared him for this time, that she would not be back? Was he with Diane or dreaded horror – Antonio! It was unbearable, sitting around, waiting for Matteo Flores to contact him.

He asked Grace if he could stay over for a few nights. Her calm presence would soothe his agitation. He was still locked out of spending too many nights at her apartment. They both needed space as he worked through his therapy sessions. He promised himself they would be living together in a permanent arrangement once he had cleared the cobwebs that had cropped up in his life. Carlos was a godsend, he gave him hope that Grace would commit to marriage and that they could have their little family.

Keefe arrived without his customary coffee for two. His

emotions were raw and his mind in a crazed concern for Carlos. His mental muddle played out various scenarios on the child's safety, leaving him confused.

'Stress with Antonio's antics could have added to Camila's rapid decline. Poor Carlos! When will we know where he is?'

'I have to contact Camila's friend, Diane. I hope Carlos' is with her, and not Antonio! There's something strange about this guy, but Carlos loves him, that was clear to me. I don't know how this will end.'

'You should go to Camila's funeral. Contact Diane as soon as possible. You need to be with Carlos now. He must feel that you are there to protect him. Poor love, I bleed for him.'

He held Grace's hands to his chest, absorbing her encouragement, taking in the moment, and mentally working through his next decision.

'Mo ghrá, as god is my witness, I will fight whoever it is for custody. I am going to bring our boy home.' His emotion-laden voice made her teary. The determination in his words held the promise that the Keefe she loved was back. That is what drew her to him, in the first place, he was not deadwood, he had a fire in him that she needed. His emotions were fragile ever since Carlos appeared in his life, not the vacuous sentimentality of his excessive drinking days.

'Do whatever it takes, I'll be right beside you.'

'Thank you, I cannot do this alone. I would be lost without you.'

As if the moment had mended his head and heart, Keefe asked, 'Is Patience okay? When is she due back home?'

This concern was his fear articulating that she would be alone once he left for Spain. Frequent departures to Spain might become a part of his life until legal matters were settled.

'She's well, but I have no definite return date from her yet.'

They spent the day together in quiet conversation until he called Diane in Granada.

The courts had placed Carlos in foster care.

Until Camila's will was read and the elected guardian was thoroughly cleared of any criminal charges and further checks for drug and alcohol dependency, Carlos would remain in foster care.

Keefe booked his flight for Monday morning to get there in time for Camila's funeral on Thursday, with the hope that he would be allowed to see Carlos before the funeral.

Grace was back on anxiety medication after Keefe left. She dreaded the pervasive thoughts of Carlos in foster care. She and Patience were aware of Felicity's horrific experience as a child in multiple foster homes. Perhaps he was with a good family. In a short space of time, Carlos had crept into her heart, the yearning to see him and touch him consumed her. With every beat of her pulse her need grew to protect, and give Keefe's son, the best childhood she could.

She called Patience to explain the situation, hoping her sister might tell her she would be home soon.

Patience was relieved when Grace told her about the airport incident. 'I was a bit surprised when I heard this from Felicity. Please don't keep anything from me. Lord knows we've been down that soul destroying path.'

Grace agreed that it was not the ideal way to handle the situation.

'You have so much on your shoulders now that I thought I would tell you when you got home.'

'I might be your baby sister, but I can handle anything,' Patience giggled.

Secrets were detrimental to their family. Varuna died, ignorant to what Grace had suffered – her silence was self-destructive until she lifted the dark veil of the abuse she suffered in South Africa. They had to maintain the bond their mothers desired, and transparency was vital for that. Grace promised to keep her updated on Keefe's situation.

Keefe's journey to Spain exhausted him. Two hours prior to his departure from Sydney, Matteo Flores sent him a message to meet as soon as he arrived. This had him churning in a relentless gyre, imagining all sorts of terrible things.

An hour after he settled in his hotel in the city centre in Granada, Matteo arrived. The hotel bar was relatively quiet for a private conversation.

'My concern is that Carlos is in a foster home. Camila will be turning in her grave.'

Matteo was surprised when Keefe refused a glass of whiskey saying water was all he wanted. His obvious concern for Carlos' welfare was the elixir Keefe needed on this cold night.

'It makes me uneasy too. Will I be allowed to see Carlos?'

'Certainly, call Diane to arrange it through my office. She is the contact person for his foster parents.'

'Thank god. I was worried it might be Antonio.'

Matteo was not at liberty to take sides although Keefe suspected his dissatisfaction with Antonio's behaviour and attitude.

'Camila requested that you be present when her will outlining her wish for Carlos' care is read.'

'Thank you for letting me know. Who is arranging her burial?'

'Diane is arranging all of that as a long-standing friend. They are... were... more like sisters.'

'Aye, I should have known that.'

'Camila wanted to be cremated. She left a letter with Diane to that effect. The reading of the will be on Wednesday morning. It's before the cremation, given the circumstances around Carlos' care. How long will you be staying?'

'I have an open ticket, but cannot stay for more than a month, I'm afraid.'

'Good, that should be enough time to see how things progress with the court decision regarding Carlos' carer. A private gathering has been arranged at the crematoria. Keep close to Diane, she will let you know more on that, and organise for you to see Carlos soon.'

Keefe was happy with the arrangement, but hated the word, 'carer,' it sounded distant and cold. He had an ally in Matteo who was now comfortable with slipping in a few Spanish words into their conversation. He spoke of his family with love and pride. He had twin boys aged five and a newborn baby girl.

'Camila will rest in peace with Carlos in your care.'

Keefe shook Matteo's hand and thanked him for coming out at an insane hour on a bitterly cold night.

On that chilly night in January he left Keefe warm with hope.

A RESTLESS NIGHT in a strange bed, sudden change of season, long distance travel, and anxiety over Carlos' care, played havoc with Keefe's emotions. He picked up the journal Grace had given him to document everything that transpired while he was in Granada.

Through his foggy thoughts all he could write was:

I am here to take my boy home.

He stopped, shut the journal, and watched the BBC News, read a few chapters on his research paper and fell asleep around 3 am.

At nine o' clock he woke with a jolt, remembering he was in Granada. He ordered a room service breakfast and called Diane. She sobbed when she heard him on the line.

'I'm glad, you've come, Keefe. I am so worried about Carlos. Camila would have hated this situation. Lord help us!'

'You have a lot to deal with, right now, Diane. Please tell me how I can help ease things for you.'

'Matteo called me early this morning to say you wanted to see Carlos. Gracias, for offering to help me. I will arrange a visit with Carlos and get back to you later today.

After she hung up, he was saddened that she would be devastated when Carlos left Spain with him. She had lost her beloved friend and now his hope to have Carlos in Sydney would leave her life empty.

He drew up a to-do list at the back of his journal, to keep track of everything. Emotional baggage left him with poor memory and Grace was not around to prompt him.

- See Carlos before the funeral
- Contact Matteo before the reading of Camila's final wishes
- Spend at least two hours each morning on research paper
- Keep Grace informed when new situations arise
- Call Aileen on Fridays with updates
- Check if Diane needs financial assistance for the cremation

He left the rest of the page blank, to slot in other things as they arose. Diane was the only friend he had in Spain, a new friend given to him by Carlos and Camila.

He took a much-needed walk to clear his head. With a scarf around his neck, he was soon warm and energised as he half-walked, half-ran up and down stairs, and around small cobbled lanes, lost in the events of recent days.

He sat on a bench overlooking the city, in full aerial view of tightly packed rooftops. He tried to immerse himself in the sights around him, but he was not here with a tourist mindset, it was not his purpose. All he saw was his son reaching out for him through the haze over the city.

Growing up for most of his life, without his father, made him appreciate why Carlos needed to have him in his life. Many families struggled with raising children after the death of a spouse as his mam had. His memory of his father was a glimmer, he was five at the time, unaffected by the grief his mother hid from him and Aileen. He saw his mother age with working two jobs to provide a good education, food and a home for them. She had bouts of bronchial illness from working at the dry-cleaners at night. Mam ensured they wanted for nothing.

He felt a warm teardrop roll down his cold cheek in this private, vulnerable moment. The past returned to add to his pain. Carlos faced a similar future in a motherless world. If it meant giving up his job in Australia to be close to Carlos, he would. Relocating to Spain was not something he desired but necessity would decide for him. He worried if that decision arose, he might lose Grace. It was a Catch-22 situation. He had to stop falling prey to such destructive thoughts, it was too much of a burden to contemplate in an already stressful situation. He whispered in his solitude, 'Mam, please guide me through this.'

He retraced his steps to the hotel. A little family of four picnicked on the grassy verge. They frolicked and laughed as the mother buttoned the children's jackets up to their chins. No sooner had she done this, the little boy pulled off his jacket, running away as he laughed the sweetest laugh that made Keefe smile. He wanted his own little family too. This was something that never crossed his mind until he looked into the curious, bright, blue eyes of Carlos Flores.

'O cruel, cruel fate!' he muttered.

Losing Grace or Carlos would be unbearable. He remembered that Nina Holstead, who introduced him to Grace at the medical conference in Amsterdam, had a sister who was a barrister in Spain. If he needed legal support, he could reel in that contact. He made a note to add this to his to-do-list. He felt safe in that Matteo Flores was rooting for him through his actions rather than his words. He would only call Nina for her sister's help if things got out of hand.

As he got closer to the hotel, a male voice behind him yelled, 'Keefe Daly! Go home!'

He spun on his heels and caught sight of a pair of stocky legs disappearing down a side street. Sweat dampened his hairline – it could only be Antonio who figured out where to find him. Should he let Matteo know? He shot that thought down, he was not injured and complaining might hurt his situation with Carlos. He had to tread carefully. Grace warned him to err on the side of caution. 'Think before you speak,' was her warning.

THE DESIRE for the sound of Grace's gentle voice killed his reason, he called her even though she was on shift that evening.

Grace picked up after several rings.

'Hey, Keefe? Everything okay?'

'Sorry to call you at work, mo ghrá, I need your soothing voice'.

'Are you okay? I am on my dinner break in fifteen minutes, may I call you back? I stepped into the office to pick up a folder when I heard my phone buzzing on my desk.'

'I'm okay? I could call you tomorrow, I'm sorry for my impulsive call.'

'I'll call you back soon, I need to hear your voice more than you know,' she laughed.

Keefe would not call her at work without a text message first, something was wrong.

She had to be strong for whatever he was about to tell her.

18

WHAT'S EATING MING XU?

Patience arranged a catch up with Ming, she was due to fly back to China the next evening. She had been unusually quiet throughout her stay at the Panna Centre. Masuyo's demands on Patience's time left no room to pursue what was eating Ming. They had drifted apart after striking up a close friendship at the camp in some godforsaken, unknown location. Contemplation Lane provided the possibility for undisturbed quality time.

'I can't believe you're leaving tomorrow. We've barely had any personal conversation these past weeks.' Patience complained.

Ming read the rock inscriptions and walked down the lane wrapped in solitude. She responded to Patience without so much as a glance.

'I suppose we have all been preoccupied with Akanya's death, investigation and then the funeral.' She sounded exhausted.

Patience proceeded, aware that Ming would retreat into a shell, shutting down any communication if she felt uncomfortable with the questions she was asked.

'How are things at your school? Was it easy getting back to work after we returned from those months at the Mission?'

'My students are good. They were delighted to have me back, so the return was easy for me. Admin was in a mess though – the old, when the cat's away story, you know. It took several weeks to wade through all the paperwork. I am eager to get back now that we've done all we could for our departed sister.'

'Yeah, your students would have welcomed you with open arms. I was fortunate that Virginia ran a shipshape routine during my absence. There's a new staff member at the SHSO office too. I'm not happy with the new woman, to be honest. She is experienced, I'll give her that, but she's slippery.' Patience spoke without stopping, suddenly aware that Ming was in her own world again.

In a distant, distracted voice, she replied, 'You must be careful with new staff. I worry when new staff arrive at my school.'

'Virginia is keeping a careful eye on her for me.' Patience decided to tackle the problem because their conversation was going nowhere with what she wanted to know.

'Ming, is everything okay? I get the feeling that something is not quite right. You can tell me to shut up, it's not my business, but I do care that you are not yourself these days. Whatever it is that's bothering you, I would like to think that I could help you.'

'I'm sorry, Patience, for being inattentive. I have a lot on my mind, personal stuff which I won't dump on you.'

With gentle coercion she explained what troubled her.

There was a visiting teacher from England at her school for a few months. He had completed a study on international schools in a few countries and had written to ask if he could come over to her school as a resident researcher or teacher. Her generous nature and passion for education sanctioned his work, and she offered him accommodation at the school. They struck up a close friendship and were still in touch even though he had returned to England.

'I'm pleased that you have an international connection now in education. I am a firm believer in networking to enhance whatever it is we're doing. But, I suspect, there's more that you're not saying, girlfriend.'

Ming's partial smile was a dead giveaway that Patience was right. She looked away as she spoke.

'I never thought it possible, that I would feel this way about someone. I convinced myself that after my wai-pu's and jia mu's lives that I would never love a man for fear of being treated the same way they were.' Ming's usual placidity was flustered. She was clearly awkward with sharing this intimate detail.

'It's wonderful that you have found love, embrace it, Ming, don't be evasive or dismissive of what you're feeling. Tell me more, I've been starved of good news and a true-life romance is exactly what I need.'

Patience's jovial manner broke the wall that had grown between them in India.

'It's complicated, not just a feel-good romance story. He wants me to move to England and to work there with him.'

She knew this would be difficult for Ming. She was committed to her school and students. It would be cutting the umbilical cord, expecting her to move to England.

'Yes, I can see how that would be a difficult decision for you. Have you thought it through? Do you have a way around it?'

'No, I don't. I can't abandon my students.'

Patience understood this stubborn adherence to passion.

'Won't you look at options, perhaps time spent in both countries. You would get the best of both worlds, that way.'

Ming looked at Patience like she had lost all reason.

'That won't work. Students would be disrupted.'

'If you have the right assistant, it will work. You lay the foundation first to make it a reality for yourself. Now, more importantly, what attracted you to the Englishman? Does he have a name?' Patience was not going to let Ming protest any more.

'I can't… it makes me sad… '

'Feeling sad is a way of addressing what's holding you back.'

'I have only ever known men who had women at their beck and call. His name's Nick Coleridge – have you noticed the improvement in my English with having him around?' Ming managed a smile.

'You have always spoken the Queen's English. Now you have a live mentor from the Queen's region!' Patience slapped Ming on the back and laughed now that they were both relaxed around each other. 'Remember the time you said you don't like the English expression, 'don't look a gift horse in the mouth.' Well, don't do that now. This is a precious time in your life.'

'I told Nick about that expression. He enjoyed it as much as you did.' It was good to hear Ming's laugh again.

'Come on, Ming, you seem to have a good connection with Nick. If you can laugh with him and share your vulnerabilities and faux pas, I reckon he comes around once in a life time. Now tell me more about the enigmatic Nick Coleridge.'

'We spent many blissful hours over cups of tea as I listened to him recite poetry. He is a poet, too, please don't say, that's corny.'

'Perfect! What's holding you back? I would love to have a poet in my life. I would be swooning over his love poems. What a life! Divide your time between England and China.'

'There's more. He's asked me to marry him. I'm petrified.'

Ming's history was the thing holding her back, but she had to give the relationship a chance, even if she did not want long-term commitment, or she would regret not doing it.

'He loves poetry, your grandmother was a poet, I feel the destiny that goes beyond romance or attraction.'

'He's helping me get wai-pu's poems, *Songs of a Stolen Heart,* published in England.'

'Great! What else attracted you to him?' It excited Patience to hear that love was possible at any age, a blissful, soulful love.

Grace found it, although there were challenges yet to be over-come. She was dying to know more about Ming's English love.

'He's a soft spoken, gentle being. He opens doors for me and looks at me like I'm the only person in the room – me, can you imagine that? I don't deserve this.'

'Ahhhh,' Patience said, rubbing her arms, 'that gave me goose bumps! How dare you say you don't deserve being valued? You must stop believing that. If there's one thing I will leave you with, it's that you should think about that marriage proposal. Give him a chance, Ming. Something tells me you won't regret it. If you don't listen to your heart you might regret it years later.'

'He is an only child, devoted to his mother, that is why he wants his home base in England.'

'This guy gets better with every sentence!'

'We talk every day, I miss him and that's odd for me. He returns to China in a month, and I know he will want an answer. I have a lot of decisions to make ...'

'Stop saying that like it's a business transaction!'

Patience told her that her life was just as important as the school and students she served. After several convincing reasons that she should give the relationship a chance, Ming nodded her head.

'I will consider it, thank you for your advice. How do I deserve a friend like you, and a man like Nick?'

Patience ached for her friend. She saw Grace go through the same feelings of inferiority, seeing herself as undeserving of the positivity of life. It was the broken who struggled more with this dilemma. Yet, they were perfect individuals in all they did.

'You have to see yourself as I see you, Ming Xu, as your students see you.'

More talking was unnecessary now. Ming held Patience's hand in hers, sitting in silent contemplation of where her life was heading.

. . .

Fear is a strange weapon, it is a self-inflicted wound, the familiar in a tormented life. It held back, it stole years, and left undiscovered cherished moments.

Patience had much to think about in her own life. Ming was touched by the magical brush of love. She lost Petros all those years ago. Pride got in the way. As much as she offered wholesome truths and dished out advice on how to put one's self first – she was sadly lacking in that area. Had she immersed herself in helping women of domestic violence to blunt her own sense of insecurity? When friends found their life partners, she was happy for them while feeling her own impending loneliness. Felicity's short-lived marriage was not futile, she got to know love, and Virginia had found a man, old enough to be her father but who loved her for who she was. Grace, darling Grace, had her 'keefer,' but life continued throwing her curves.

She had to keep going to stop herself from being sad about what her fate would have been in the love department. That night she was bombarded by dreams. She was a teenager in South Africa, walking beside Petros on a sun-drenched beach. Clouds gathered, shadows closed in on her – Grace was walking away, her back to her, together with a child and a man, holding hands. All three were fading in the distance. Perspiration prickled on her neck, she tried to call out, her throat was dry, her call went unheard. She awoke, bathed in sweat, confused by her disturbing visions, desperate for air and a drink of water.

Outside her bedroom window, she caught sight of two figures in the garden. Deepak and Hiyana appeared to be in an argument. He was motionless, her arms were flying around, trying to emphasise some point. She wished she could hear the gist of their argument.

Here, in Panna, the two young people she had much hope for,

were not happy. Another dimension of stress was added to the promises she made to herself and the Mission.

Selflessness was a lonely world.

19

A SIEGE

Grace slipped back to her old pattern, immersing herself in her work to the exclusion of everything else. She struggled to relinquish dependency on sleeping pills. Loneliness and sadness crept in with Patience and Keefe out of the country, work was her safety net to numb the void. Her general reclusive nature invited her one and only good friend, Andrew Lang into her space but he too felt she had walled off part of herself from him, in recent weeks.

The summer was intense, the heat somehow encouraged more violent acts of aggression. The number of serious injuries had trebled, and Dr Romero had to be summoned to lend a hand on the nights he was not rostered for duty. Friday and Saturday nights were no longer an option as free evenings for Grace, those were the busiest nights of the season.

Andrew kept a close watch over her, giving her space but aware that she needed to be reminded to take a break. She was vulnerable in her private life and strong for those she served. His life was less complicated these days, he had himself to care for and accepted that Grace would never look at him the way she looked at Keefe. That they could still have a friendship and a wonderful working relationship was enough to keep him happy.

In another life, in her younger years, she would take him for better or for worse. Now during their ER shifts there was no time for coffee breaks or a quick catch up between cuts, bruises, cleaning, stitching and rushing patients off for surgery. ER had become a production line in the mending of human bodies, and a few souls. Adrenaline, testosterone aggression created senseless acts of inhumanity that multiplied with each passing year. If only the world paused, contemplated, or meditated for inner calm, so many lives could be spared. This had become Grace's daily mantra. Alcohol and increased drug abuse played a fair part in the clashes amongst young men and women. She thought of parents who had to endure this, living on the edge, fearing the behaviour of their children. Parenting was difficult in a world of easy access.

AT AROUND 11 pm a seriously injured young man with stab wounds to his upper torso and cuts on his face, arrived. A family brawl had left him unresponsive. He had lost much blood. His body temperature was dangerously low. Nurse Hobbs and Dr Romero worked on him with no success and decided he had to be taken to theatre, stitching the wound did not stop his blood loss. Andrew took over the care of the patient to free Dr Romero to assist paramedics upon arrival.

The young man's mother's relentless wail that her son was going to die distressed other patients waiting for medical attention. Her dramatic behaviour in throwing herself on the ground, then the young man, with her, would help her to her feet, and down she would go again. The woman's disruption was more than Grace could bear. She asked the young man to take the woman out of the waiting room if she did not pull herself together. He grew hostile to Grace's request.

'Why are you picking on my aunty, huh? She is stressed about my cousin. What if he dies? Try to be kind.'

Grace was flabbergasted by his aggressive outburst.

'We are doing the best we can for him. His injuries are severe, and his mother must remain calm if we need her to talk to him.'

The woman wailed louder when Grace advised that she might need a sedative. The young man yanked his aunt's arm, mumbling and cursing under his breath.

'Let's go outside, aunty. This crazy doctor wants to drug you.' His menacing look sent a cold ripple through Grace.

The woman refused to move. He lifted her like a rag doll, glared at Grace again and stepped outside.

ER's swing doors danced in perpetual motion that night with many entrances and few exits.

Andrew tapped Grace's arm, 'A private word please.'

Andrew's serious look conveyed that things had not gone as expected. 'Have we lost him,' she whispered.

'Yes, just about three minutes ago. He was brought in too late, he lost a lot of blood. He went into cardiac arrest and did not recover.' Andrew was trembling. It was the first time, after singularly treating a patient, he had a patient die.

'Leave it to me, Andrew. The mother will not take this too well. She is already beside herself, creating quite a disturbance. You take a moment in the office, I will speak to the young man with her.'

Andrew headed to the office, drew the blinds and released his anger and frustration. He questioned what else he could have done to have saved the patient, pondered over the process he followed, when suddenly there was a loud thud and the office door burst open with the forceful kick from a heavy boot. Grace called out, 'Hang on, you can't go in there, that's a staff-only area.' A scowling enraged young man lunged at Andrew – he threw him to the ground with a switch blade ready for action.

'Call yourself a doctor, you... useless piece of crap.... What do you know about saving lives!' He was desperate to get the pointy end of the blade into Andrew's neck. Grace called the police with the wailing mother standing beside her. The young man held Andrew down with his foot, and turned to lunge at Grace. Andrew stretched forward and grabbed his legs, too late, he felt a sting in his neck, followed by a ringing sound in his ears, then blacked out. Dr Romero ran into the office, shoved Grace out of harm's ways as police arrived to handcuff the young man whose snarling rage was beyond any of their control.

'Murderers! How can you call yourselves doctors!'

Dr Romero attended to Andrew. He had deep lacerations on his arms and left shoulder, and one on his chest where the knife had ripped his gown. Grace made an urgent announcement over the intercom, 'Dr down! Dr down!' This was their internal messaging code for more staff to assist with incoming patients in ER during a commotion.

In over a decade as head of ER, Grace had never had a doctor, or anyone attacked by a patient. Andrew spoke of such situations and she stopped him from having negative thoughts. He was rushed off to theatre, leaving her feeling weak from the sudden turn of events. She had to push on, many patients needed attention.

Three hours later a groggy, smiling Andrew was wheeled into Grace's office.

'Andrew, how are you doing? I am so sorry this happened. I should have seen this coming. The young man was quite aggressive earlier in the evening.' Grace breathed a sigh of relief to see him up and about, but a tad too soon.

'I'll live, Dr Sharvin.' Andrew laughed, not feeling any pain. With the anaesthetic still in his bloodstream he was floating, weightless and confused, 'no need to be sorry, darling, it's the nature of the job at times, my love.'

'Oh dear, you need to sleep off the effect of the anaesthetic.' He would no doubt be embarrassed if he knew he was loud enough to be heard by patients, sounding somewhat like an amorous drunk.

'I should not have berated the mother's behaviour, this might have angered your assailant.'

'Well, his brother or friend dying was entirely my fault, so you are redeemed, Dr Sharvin!' Andrew began sobbing, his out of control, overly relaxed body exposed his vulnerability. Grace looked over at a smiling Dr Romero.

'Dr Romero, what have you administered to my colleague? He is still very groggy, I think he should be sent home to sleep it off.'

'It would be better for him to remain here until the effects wear off. He might be in a lot of pain when it does.' Dr Romero suggested.

He ordered a bed and told Grace all should be well with Andrew in a few hours. Dr Romero took charge of the situation more than once that evening. His calm and confident medical manner did not go unnoticed. Both Nurse Hobbs and Dr Romero who came in as trainees to her facility were showing great promise. From her early days as head of ER, and the resistance she faced from some staff who cruelly labeled her the 'ice maiden,' she was now surrounded by passionate, competent medics, and that was all she could have hoped for.

Andrew spent the night in ER and left with Grace in the morning. She insisted he stay at her place until he felt well enough to return to his apartment. With minimum protest from him, she made him comfortable in Patience's old room. After breakfast and a painkiller, he fell asleep, she called Keefe.

He chose not to tell her about his incident outside the hotel. She was anxious about Carlos being in foster care so Keefe settled on recounting his visit.

'Mo ghrá, Carlos remembered me, he ran to me, grabbing my legs, asking to be picked up. He placed his head on my shoulder and would not move!' His concern that Carlos would spurn him was not his reality. She heard the warmth and excitement in his voice, this was what they both needed to feel whole again.

'That's just wonderful, Keefe! What are the foster parents like?'

'They seem good, aye, they are. But they have six other children ranging from eighteen to Carlos as the youngest. He has been used to undivided attention from Camila, so I'm not sure how good the situation is for him.'

He explained that Diane arranged the visit and that the foster parents were present for the entirety of his visit. He also expressed his concern that Carlos howled when he left, begging him not to leave.

'He called me, papi, mo ghrá. I've got to get cracking with the paperwork here after Camila's last wishes are read. I'm not nervous about that as Matteo Flores indicated I had nothing to worry about. It's Antonio's reactions that concern me.'

She wished him well and told him about Andrew's incident in ER. He told Grace it was about time she went into private practice as the social landscape was notorious in recent years.

'The situation that arose last night could happen anywhere, it's the reality of life these days.'

He insisted she consider how much longer she was going to stay on as head of ER and thanked her for advising him to document his experience in Spain. They parted, hopeful, and happy that the custody matters would soon be resolved.

She was working on a joint paper with Keefe on alternate therapies for the terminally ill. She poured another cup of coffee, got comfy in the soft folds of her favourite couch and tapped out her findings and thoughts on her laptop.

The mind was powerful in supporting the terminally ill to manage pain. Music, poetry recital, reading, listening to motivational talks and enjoying comedy shows and a host of other activities were drawn into her paper. Going down a different path when medical intervention was no longer a viable option for some patients, appealed to her. They hoped that what they researched could be cited in medical journals with the prospect of writing a book on the various therapies they were testing.

She had a little notebook in the hallway dresser draw with her mother's list of healing spices. She was an advocate for natural medicine. Grace hoped to consult with an Ayurvedic doctor when they were ready to pool their research before publishing the book.

She looked around her apartment and longed for a garden she could call her own. With that thought she dozed off into a peaceful sleep with the sun streaming in from the balcony.

20

STIRRINGS

Patience was not going to leave India without an understanding of why it appeared that Hiyana and Deepak were arguing late the night before. The future of the Panna Centre depended on its younger generation, and if they lacked integrity or could not work together, it was best that they were asked to leave. She knew this tough love approach had to be adopted. A thought on Lindiwe Johnson, her own staff who sold her out to the media, surfaced. She had to take a stronger stand with her when she got back to Australia.

Amidst the difficulties ahead, she was delighted to receive word that Azmil planned to visit her in India. With much weighing on her mind, these days, news of his promise to visit excited her. Hiyana brought her a hot, freshly brewed cup of coffee, just the way she liked it. Her usual exuberance was absent that morning, her eyes were red, and her smile a passing shadow. Patience snatched the moment to pry for reasons on what happened under a hot moonlit Indian sky. Although she protested being served this way, it provided the opportunity to corner her. She knew the young woman to be intelligent enough to evade situations in ingenious ways. Hiyana, in many ways a strategist, used her mind or beauty to gain the information she wanted – she was a victim to Patience's sleuthing. A young female politician, in the making, up against a seasoned woman whose life experience crossed international borders.

'Good morning, Hiyana. Thank you, that coffee smells great! How are you this morning? You look tired. Are you unwell?'

Patience wormed her way in like a probing prosecution attorney. Her *tell me all, tell me now* curiosity kicked into gear. Hiyana flinched, aware that her façade was not impenetrable.

'Good morning, sister Patience, I'm better for seeing you. I am a little tired, the heat kept me up.'

Little liar, Patience thought. The heat had no impact on her, she was used to it, having lived all her life in India.

'I love seeing you, but don't like that you have to serve me, so how about getting yourself a cup of coffee and joining me for a quiet morning.'

Hiyana hesitated, 'I have a lot to do this morning, the floors need to be mopped, and students' meals prepared.'

'I'll ask Ojala to allow you an hour out of work, get your coffee and come back.' Patience took on a stern school teacher tone to ensure that she returned without squirming her way out.

Hiyana thanked her with acute suspicion that something was amiss. She returned five minutes later.

'I'm going to miss having you around when I return home. We need more time like this to get to know each other better. I hope you know, when I meet people, I don't forget them, but keep in touch. So, are you game to have an 'Aunty' in your life?' Patience laughed to ease Hiyana's obvious nervousness.

'It is a privilege and honour to call you my aunty.' She smiled, 'perhaps someday I will venture out of India and visit you in Australia.'

With a comfortable air settling between them, and a few sips of coffee down, Patience was ready to strike.

'Hiyana, I hope you don't mind me saying this, but something seems different about you this morning. Are you sure there is nothing troubling you? If you think I'm being inquisitive, you can tell me to shut up.'

'Oh, my goodness, I could never tell you to shut up, that will be most disrespectful of me. Kanya-ma would turn in her grave if I did that.' She quickly slipped in, 'By the way, why do we say,'turn in her grave' when ma was cremated?'

Patience laughed and accepted that Hiyana was a young woman who was curious about the world and its workings, but also a clever tactician in avoiding her question.

'Technically her ashes are buried in her mother's and sister's shared grave, so the word, 'buried' is not altogether wrong.'

Hiyana nodded and accepted Patience's explanation.

'To be truthful, I am a little stressed. May I speak about a personal matter with you, as one would with an aunty?'

'Go ahead, I'm all ears, but are you absolutely sure you want me to know what it is that's on your mind?'

Two strategists pitted their skills against each other for the truth.

'When Kanya-ma came back from the training camp, where you both met, she insisted we adhere to Truth, Understanding and Compassion as our values. She said we did most of the time, but had to be conscious about following it to the letter. You live this too, sister, or should I say aunty?'

'That is sound advice, a rose my dear Hiyana is just as sweet, so sister or aunty I shall be!'

'You know Shakespeare too, I love his plays!'

'Who doesn't, a man for all seasons of life.'

'It's like I'm in one of his tragedies right now. I will appreciate your honest opinion.'

Patience listened, concerned that what she might have seen from her bedroom window was far more serious than she had anticipated.

'I'm intrigued now.'

'What is the appropriate age for a woman to be married in the West?'

'Now, I'm not the wisest, nor qualified in that department,' Patience giggled, 'give me some context to respond in a meaningful way for you.'

'An estimate, your first reaction, is all I need to know.'

'Any age, then, if it feels right, provided the person is not a child, or forced into a marriage. Those would signal alarm bells for me.'

'What about my age?'

'I would suggest that getting an education first is important at your age, although there's nothing wrong with having a love interest around. Commitment is what I would be wary of at your age.'

'Can you tell me why you say not to commit at my age to a partner?'

'I think we all evolve over time, what I might feel at eighteen is not necessarily what I might still think and feel at twenty-five.'

'Are you saying that love is changeable?'

'Ahhhh... that's a hard one, I don't know. The mind changes in how we perceive the world, which may, it just may, impact on relationships, with life partners that is. We don't stop loving our families, we accept who they are as we have always known them. With a partner, I believe, if you are not like-minded, there could be challenges along the way.'

'That makes sense. Thank you. Now I will give you my context.'

Patience was awed by this clever way in which Hiyana extracted her views before she shared her personal dilemma. For her young self, she knew how to articulate her thoughts without impetuosity. A politician was embedded somewhere within her, a good politician. Many shot from the hip, making idiots of themselves in a public sphere through ridiculous speeches or by posting incendiary tweets. In this moment she believed, with the

Mission's grooming, Hiyana had what it would take to lead a nation.

'It's Deepak, sister, he is, the 'man' in question. He has asked me to marry him and I told him just what you said, that I wanted to gain my university qualification first, then I was free to think about marriage. We are not in a relationship. He is a tad old-fashioned, a village boy, you know, so he follows his grandfather's ways. I escaped what would have been a hellish marriage and do not want to make the same mistake. Don't get me wrong, Deepak is a wonderful guy.'

She had it all worked out and was not in want of any advice. All that she required was someone to listen to her thoughts, just as Patience and Grace needed in tricky situations.

'Do you love Deepak, Hiyana?'

After a momentary pause.

'I don't know. I enjoy his company, his gentle nature and respectful ways. We are opposites in many ways, that's good for a permanent relationship, right?'

'It might be to avoid tedium and the boredom of feeling like you're married to yourself!'

They shared a hearty laugh on the serious topic of love and marriage.

'Without having all the answers, I would say, it's not worth putting off love, to live a life of regret thereafter, although some lucky people find love again.'

Hiyana's coy look and lowered tone put Patience in a corner, inviting her to unveil her private life.

'Have you known such love, sister?'

'I did but did not have the courage to let it materialise and will never know how it could have been because he was killed.'

A long awkward pause followed. Patience contained her emotions, and Hiyana had a revelation with that intimate detail.

'How very sad! I believe, this is indeed my answer. Your life answers what I need to do.'

'How so, what will you do?'

'I can't marry Deepak now, but I can return his love. If it's not meant to be, I'll be open to another love. This does not make me an untamed woman like culture dictates, it will make me true to who I am, my authentic self. Awesome!'

Patience was unsure if she might have inadvertently encouraged the pursuit of endless lovers in this overzealous reaction.

'Only ever do what is right for you, what speaks true to you. Think about why you joined the centre here, why did you run away, and what did you run from to guide your future decisions?'

'Yes, I am not prepared to marry now. If this makes Deepak unhappy, so be it, he can still have a good friend in me if he so chooses.'

'Well, my dear Hiyana... if he cannot wait for you, or respect your decision, then don't waste your time and your beautiful soul on him.'

'He was very upset with me last night, saying that I might meet someone else while I'm away studying, if we marry, he does not have to worry about that, as I will be his. Silly crazy boy love talk you know.'

'To be quite blunt, that's his issue not yours. Get on with the business of educating yourself.'

Hiyana was grateful for Patience's frank advice and said she would chat to Ojala too. She needed a sister to share her load. Patience ticked a few more boxes in Hiyana's favour. She decided to tap into her views on leadership at the centre.

'I have a question for you.'

'Anything sister, what is it?'

'If I asked you if you could run the Panna Centre as its leader, what would you say?'

'I'm not ready. One day, I would love to, only when I feel equipped to do so.'

'Thank you for your honest response. You have what it takes, is my opinion. Let time do the trick.'

They walked together to the dining room where Deepak was setting up for breakfast. Patience caught the love and admiration in his soft brown eyes when he saw Hiyana. She felt a stirring within, in remembrance of Petros. Nobody could fill the space he left, no one. She had chosen to shut herself off from love and had no idea how to change that.

21

CARLOS

The reading of Camila's last wish went through without a hitch.

KEEFE WAS GRANTED full custodial rights over Carlos. Her impassioned declaration was that her son should be raised by his biological father. Carlos deserved what she was denied.

Antonio had no rights – no claim whatsoever and a categorical refusal of any visitation rights. She included a supporting document outlining her reasons which was not read that morning. His absence at the reading, suggested he was aware that he had been excluded.

Keefe made the sign of the cross as an instinctive act of gratitude and hope that Antonio would comply with Camila's wish. She was a private person, guarded about who she was intimate with on Carlos' background. How did someone like her end up with someone like Antonio, is what bothered Keefe. Some men avoided women who were single parents, perhaps Antonio was the only one she found... he tossed the thought aside, it was unkind to Camila's memory.

Diane was allowed visitation rights and when Carlos was a responsible young man, he would be allowed to travel to Spain to visit Diane, without Keefe. He accepted that it was Camila's fair acknowledgement of love, and respect for Diane who stood by her in all the years he was ignorant of Carlos' birth. He hated that a DNA test had to prove his paternity. How would he explain this to the adult Carlos without appearing to be a reckless man, and father?

He thanked Matteo Flores for the fair and transparent handling of Camila's last wishes. Keefe asked how long the court would take to sanction his full custody of Carlos and was surprised by Matteo's explanation. Spanish law stated that when Carlos was thirteen, there would be a court hearing to determine if he wished to continue living with his father. He was quick to add that by the time Carlos turned thirteen, the law on that might be altered. This did not perturb Keefe, he was going to do everything within his power to ensure that Carlos loved him, and never wanted to leave him.

Ninety days was the time frame from the initial lodgement to the final signing, this stressed him knowing he had to go back to Australia and return closer to the final days.

Fear skulked in the depths of his soul, what if there was resistance from Carlos when it was time to take him home? Children thrived in consistent environments. Warmth, love, routine was the point of comfort and security, a necessity to survival. Would Carlos spurn him at that time?

Grace spent her days figuring out ways to ensure that Carlos was not anxious with all the changes in his little life. His welfare was paramount.

'You can't leave him in foster care. Will Diane be willing to babysit him until you can bring him home. We could ask Felicity to try her influence with the courts there for an earlier signing of the papers.'

'Aye, that is the best solution, but I don't want to burden Diane with Carlos' care, and I'm not sure if the courts will grant permission to her to mind him for me.'

'I don't see why they won't, you forget she was appointed care-giver of the child during his mother's hospitalisation. Which government won't be happy with cost-cutting in removing Carlos from foster care?'

'Aye, a valid point, mo ghrá. I can't think clearly these days. I fear so much that Antonio is going to interfere in our lives.'

His head and chest were a constant ache in recent weeks, it was good to have Grace's wise processing in everything that had erupted in his world. Negativity was corrosive, he was constantly restless and confused when he needed clarity to make the right decisions for their future.

'I have to think through how I should approach Diane.'

'You will be surprised, she will be happy to oblige. Perhaps wait until after the funeral to broach this with her.'

THE FUNERAL WAS placid and simple, just as Camila presented in life – no Antonio to disturb the peace. Carlos sat between Keefe and Diane, falling asleep, oblivious to what was happening.

Lunch was arranged at Camila's favourite pub – the same pub where they had met almost five years ago before his life changed in a way he had never expected. After the guests left, Keefe remained with Diane, she needed another drink. She struggled to come to terms with Camila's death even though her friend had prepared her for the final moment. Camila was her anchor as her best friend and confidant. She was sad and lonely. Although the timing was inappropriate, Keefe had to ask the question – would she take care of Carlos until he could return, with the court's permission, to take him home to Australia? He told her he would pay for the care of all Carlos' needs. Just as Grace indicated, she was delighted to be asked to care for her best friend's son. It gave her purpose and would keep her connected to Camila's memory.

'Trust that I will do whatever it takes to make Carlos feel as loved and cared for as his mother did.' She explained that Camila had made financial provisions for Carlos' care, and that payment from Keefe was unnecessary.

A weight had been lifted, it was the emotional aspect of child-rearing that concerned him. Children formed bonds easily. He would consult with Matteo Flores on the legality of the arrangement between him and Diane. He lived for the moment when he could finally take Carlos to Australia. He was guilty for not telling Grace he was accosted on the street outside his hotel – he had promised never to conceal anything again. His concern was that her anxiety elevated each time a problem cropped up.

Lord knows he was desperate for a drink. He walked to the high street pub with a cap pulled down over his ears. He did not want to be identified if he let himself down in public. At the pub entrance, he hesitated, walked in and panicked, then dashed back down the street – he had responsibilities, he could not lose Carlos in a moment of reckless temptation. He had a medical paper to work on to add to Grace's research. He would drown himself in that, a drink, one then many would be his undoing, and dear God, Grace would never forgive him, not this time.

Someone lunged at him from behind as he sprinted back to his hotel. He heard a familiar voice and felt hot, foul breath on his ear.

'You and Diane better watch out, Carlos is my boy! He needs me, if you mess things up, who knows what I might do?'

Keefe found the strength to retaliate.

'I am acting in accordance with the law. You certainly aren't! I will charge you with harassment. Leave me alone!'

Antonio punched Keefe on the back of the head and ran off. He fell to the ground, blood trickled from his nose, he was dazed.

A sharp, tinny sound exploded in his ears, deafening him, forcing him to lie on the ground for a while. He dragged himself up, propped his body against the wall, and shuffled back to his hotel.

He cleaned up his face, nursed the back of his head with an ice swaddled towel. He popped a few painkillers in anticipation of a massive headache. Matteo had to be informed on the matter.

'Santo cielo! I don't believe this man, he's crazy, he could be locked away for this. I need to see you, to get you to a doctor and take a few photos of your injuries. The hotel surveillance recording will be used as evidence. What were you doing out at that time?'

Keefe paused, riddled with guilt, and lied, 'I needed air and took a walk up the street. The air conditioning makes me restless.'

'Another thing, Diane told me she has been receiving a spate of threatening calls, referring to her as a child snatcher. It's a woman's voice which must be someone Antonio is using to do his dirty business.'

Leaving Carlos in Spain was becoming a living nightmare.

'I don't know what Camila saw in the man, to be honest. She must have been lonely.' Matteo lamented. 'Proceed with caution, Keefe, we don't know what we're dealing with. I will have a police officer outside your hotel. You must report the incident to the police ASAP.'

'Would they believe a foreigner?'

'Trust me, when you mention Antonio, they will be all ears.'

This bit of information that Matteo left unfinished, no details provided, had Keefe more stressed than ever.

The next morning Diane came over to see him. She was afraid to call him from home, she believed her calls were tapped.

'Who did this to you?' She was shocked that Keefe's eyes were bloody, puffy and part of his face, spotted with purplish blood clots.

'Antonio did. I must report this to the police today.'

'May I accompany you there to let them know about my calls?'

'I think we should not be viewed as colluding against Antonio, it's best you go later in the day.'

'Si, you're right. I understand. Keefe, can you stay until the courts have cleared everything for you to take Carlos to Australia?'

Diane was a mess, fearful that Carlos might be snatched from her. The threatening telephone calls disturbed her. Keefe needed Felicity's advice on the matter. He trusted Matteo Flores, he needed another legal ear on the matter, to settle his own restlessness.

Granada, Melbourne and Sydney converged in assisting Keefe with the best way forward to avoid violence or abduction. Felicity suggested twenty-four-seven police guard outside Diane's apartment, with a bodyguard if she needed to leave the apartment with Carlos.

Aileen offered financial assistance with all the people Keefe had to employ to keep his son safe. He could count on Aileen for anything he needed, mam ensured that she looked out for her little brother.

With everything in place with the help of the caring people in his life, Keefe went to the foster parents' home to let them know that Diane would collect Carlos as soon as she received clearance from the court. It was expected to be a seven day wait. For the first time he could be alone with Carlos.

Carlos clung to him, nestling his head in the crook of his father's neck, like a scared little boy. Too many changes in his little life made him fretful. Keefe kissed him and whispered, 'I will be back to take you to Australia soon. Would you like that?'

Carlos nodded and whispered back, 'Want to go now, papi, go now with you.'

Those words were music to his ears, he had to keep Carlos holding onto that thought.

'Soon my darling boy, soon.'

They sat on the floor playing with Carlos' toys. He had Carlos laughing at his antics as he rolled on the floor pretending to be a car, then a dog and anything that would delight his boy.

At 4 pm that afternoon, Keefe flew out of Spain, leaving his son behind, but taking the hope that soon he will be enjoying similar fun-filled days with Carlos in Australia. A few short months ago, his life was different. The future held promise, and that was all that mattered now.

A little boy tucked away in Granada had stolen his heart, giving him renewed breath.

22

AN UNSETTLING MESSAGE

Azmil arrived at the Panna Centre at noon on Wednesday afternoon. Hiyana prepared a simple vegetarian meal at Patience's request. Azmil, she recalled, was a minimalist when it came to food as in most things, but books he devoured in large quantities. The centre continued to observe vegetarian days as an extended mark of mourning for Akanya.

Patience watched him walk up the long footpath as she did over a month ago. He wore a long, white cotton kaftan, suitable for the Indian summer heat. He waved frantically, squinting in the sun when he saw her approach. His smiling face, not quite hidden behind the beard he sported, was a welcome sight.

'Wonderful to see you, Assalamu Alaikum, sister! How are you?' He called out, speeding up his pace towards her.

Patience returned the greeting, she had profound respect for Azmil's adherence to his culture and spirituality.

'Mualaikumsalam, brother Azmil, wonderful to see you too, I am very well, thank you, and you?'

She had the urge to hook her arm through his in sisterly affection. He understood and appreciated her warmth and exuberance. She chose instead to touch his arm gently in acknowledgement of her joy in seeing him again.

'I am so excited that you have come to India while I am still here.'

'I grabbed the opportunity to see you because you were so close by, and to get some insight on another centre, through your eyes. India is my neighbour and I've never been here, before. I haven't been anywhere, really – just an armchair traveller, my whole life.' He smiled with his glowing aquamarine eyes.

'I'll show you around soon, get settled first. There are some lovely young folk I want to introduce you to. Deepak will take care of whatever you need while you're here.'

Azmil was amazed at how comfortable Patience was, almost as if she had been in Panna for many years.

Deepak ran a bath for him and Hiyana set up the dining room for an early dinner. A delicious, spicy, vegetable biriyani with split pea lentils and pickles were served that evening. Hiyana made a chilled drink of milk, almonds and sweet basil seeds into a refreshing, tasty Falooda drink. Azmil explained the benefits of the drink and the cooling effect of the seeds. Patience said it was a liquid ice cream, or a milkshake with a taste of India. Everyone laughed at her apt description of the chilled, delicately flavoured drink.

When Patience asked after Maimoona, Azmil's pride was clear.

'She has done very well. After her first round of training, she is working in a corporate industry, in Karachi, to advance her leadership and social skills.'

'I certainly saw her potential when we first met at the orphanage.'

Deepak and Hiyana listened in awe to what Maimoona had achieved.

'What are your plans for yourself, Azmil?'

'Good news – I will be going to Australia with Akbar's daugh-

ters, to help them settle in so I might see you again, down under.'
He laughed pointing to the ground.

'What do you mean, that you *might* see me in Australia, you
have to meet my family when you're there.'

'Thank you, I will certainly need some advice from you on
settling them in. It will be the blind leading the blind.' He chuckled, nodding in acknowledgement of Deepak's and Hiyana's
attentiveness to all that he said.

'My assistant, Virginia, is getting married soon, so my home
will be available for you and Akbar's daughters if they choose to
live and study in Sydney. I hope you like dogs because Sprite and
Ajax rule the roost.'

'You are very kind, I will come to Sydney to see you, the
Opera House and The Harbour Bridge! Dogs are another story,
but if they are yours and not the mangy dogs I have seen in my
life, I'm sure I will come to love them!' Hiyana and Deepak
enjoyed the humour, giggling like children.

'You are an Aussie icon, now, sister Patience,' Hiyana said,
nudging Patience on the arm.

'You better believe it!' Patience had them all laughing again
with her dramatic bow. It was good to have new company. The
stress and strain of the past weeks seemed to melt with Azmil
there.

'I believe those sights are more stunning when seen with the
naked eye.'

'I'll leave you to be the judge of that. I will gladly act as your
tour guide.'

The once, silent, aloof Azmil had grown fond of her. For all
his struggles, she found him a kindred spirit. He brought light
and laughter to the Panna Centre. She now had a claim to a
brother for the first time in her life. Akbar was a father figure to
her. She was certain about that.

Deepak enjoyed having male company at the centre. They
took long walks and spoke at length about the state of the world.

Azmil returned inspired by Contemplation Lane, softly reciting Rumi's lines on pain being messages that should be felt.

Patience knew that his pain stemmed from the loss of both parents. He was cheated from knowing them.

'I hope to someday find my father's family. It won't be easy, but I intend to find the connection. I need to know him, if you know what I mean, to make him real in my memory.'

'No doubt your parents would have been very proud of you.' Patience said with truth, understanding and compassion.

He was eternally grateful for the life Akbar had given him. Patience added that she too was saved, together with her mother, by Varuna. Her life would have taken a different trajectory had it not been for the Sharvin family.

Deepak and Hiyana suggested inviting the students for a game of charades with Azmil. His knowledge of the world had everyone in awe of how, as one who had never left his home country, he knew so much. He was a walking encyclopedia with detailed knowledge on women's rights issues, Brexit and whether technology would lead to Huxley's *A Brave New World.* He encouraged reading as the single most important activity in understanding the world. Being around youth energised Azmil and Patience. Conversations slipped well into the night. Ojala allowed the students to sit with Azmil for as long as they wanted. His inspiration came around once in a life time. That night the Pakistan-India divide melted as young people were drawn together in shared acceptance.

The next morning at breakfast, Patience and Azmil resumed their deep conversation when he revealed that he was prepared for change. He asked Akbar to appeal to the Mission to place him anywhere in the world to assist with their program. If he was accepted, he would request the United States. That would allow him to conduct his own investigation on his father's family.

Patience understood a restless spirit. She returned to South Africa for a prolonged stay, to reconnect with her clan and culture. Then her time at the Mission, in an unknown location, contributed to her now changed life. Her concern was that Azmil was of an easy nature, much like her – he could get swallowed by the Mission's demands once they had recruited him.

He had started his memoir on growing up a mixed-raced child in Pakistan. He was explicit on his struggles, wanting to ensure that others could connect to the pain and hardship he underwent.

'My mixed-race awareness came through the cruelty of the children in my class. They would have got this from their parents that I was an American bastard child.'

Patience felt the pain in those words, she experienced this growing up with Grace's family – the world outside the Sharvin home was cruel to her. Unlike Azmil, who had no siblings, she had Grace who came to her rescue every time. The destructiveness of bullying seemed odd to her when Azmil lived in a male prized society.

He recalled a glass bottle being hurled at him by teenage boys outside the school. They referred to him as 'Awara Kutta!' He asked Akbar why he was given such a label. All he diplomatically got from Akbar was that it probably occurred as a result of his fair skin. He recalled being resistant to such an explanation.

'But baba there are many fair-skinned people here.' He pushed Akbar for the truth and never forgot what he was told.

'Your mother, may she rest in peace, was Pakistani and your father was from the American air force, stationed in Peshawar. Both, very sadly, passed, leaving you without parents. Your father died before you were born.'

He said he placed Akbar in a predicament when he asked, 'Who killed them, baba? Did they die because of forbidden love?'

Akbar told him his father was killed by rebels and that his mother went missing eighteen months later. Her body was never found. He begged to know whether a possibility existed that she might be alive. His eyes glowed when he remembered asking that question and then hearing Akbar say, 'I don't think she is, Azmil.'

'That would have been a painful confirmation for you, Azmil. Akbar could not lie to you and give you false hope.'

'Yes, it stung, it stung as if I heard the sad news for the first time. I mourned my loss that day and have every day since.'

Empathy healed the moment. Words were not necessary when compassion created understanding in grief.

Patience shared her fear of being in Varuna's home, in the early days. She felt her difference, that she imposed on herself. The early days in a large house made her feel small and lost. She was born in a pokey shack, with no running water and electricity. The sudden change was overwhelming, but so was the love she received from Grace and Varuna.

They spoke of gratitude for their adoptive families who showed them the light to a better self. In that revealing moment, Patience hugged Azmil – they were similar souls, bonded as family by their circumstances.

Deepak walked in on them, awkward by their demonstration of affection. He coughed to announce his presence.

'Brother, sir, there is a lady on the telephone for you.'

AZMIL RETURNED, red-faced, frowning almost unaware that Patience and Deepak were looking at him. His aquamarine eyes were dark, the glow had vanished.

'Has something happened, Azmil?' Patience whispered, afraid to disturb him any more than he already was. Her pulse pounded in her neck as she waited for his response.

He lifted his head – fear, pain, and confusion all too clear in his face.

'Akbar baba has not returned home from the Well Study Centre since last night, that was Maa Zenab on the telephone. There was a rebel raid in the area. He stayed on after the students left, thankfully they left before the raid. He had some work he wanted done before morning. He is not answering his phone and she is afraid to send her daughters out to check on him. Calling the police is out of the question.'

'What if he is injured, or has fallen ill, and in need of medical attention?'

'Maa Zenab is aware of the secrecy around the Mission and won't breach it as Akbar baba told her never to feel pressurised to do so.'

The organisation controlled their lives even during times when lives were at risk. Patience began to accept that the Mission needed to redefine its understanding of selflessness.

23

NEW HOME

Grace's apartment was far from ideal to raise a child. She had no intention of adopting children when her biological clock ticked past her childbearing days. Her professional life consumed her fertile years. She was determined that Carlos should have a childhood home that was safe, away from the deafening sounds of congested traffic, and concrete balconies suspended in mid-air. He needed wide natural spaces just as she and Patience enjoyed as children.

She rang real estate agents and scanned the internet for the next auction and panoramic views of houses she might be keen to purchase. She loved the inner city but that was only good for a busy professional life. Her apartment held dear memories of her mother, but the time had come to move on. She intended leasing the apartment, maintaining it as her investment property, and perhaps a place to return to in later years. Patience was too far away for a second opinion. Virginia came to the rescue as another opinion into the home she intended to buy.

Keefe was back at work, he covered longer shifts. A colleague who stood in for him while he was in Spain, was on leave. Grace appreciated that he did not interfere in her choice of home for Carlos. He was thankful that she finalised this on her own.

She headed out early one Saturday morning with Virginia in tow, to the auction of a property in a lovely cul-de-sac in St Ives. The sprawling backyard was perfect for an energetic little boy. With house prices down in recent months, she had a wider reach. A five bedroom house was the least she would settle for. There had to be a room each, for Aileen and Patience, for when they stayed over. Varuna's daughter had it all planned, no loved one was going to be left out of the equation.

The leafy avenues, well-trimmed hedges and colourful, kempt gardens had oodles of eye appeal. She could see herself taking walks down the tree-lined streets to enjoy the aesthetic landscape. The house itself was an impressive building tucked in the inner corner of the cul-de-sac. The front entrance was narrow, obscuring the wide space behind it. The backyard was encircled by the building that rolled across both sides of the yard. This pleased her as it offered the safety and security of a secluded backyard. A swimming pool lay at the far end of the yard, in a Balinese setting, with a gazebo beside it, and an outdoor shower and toilet. Above the bathroom was a one bedroom granny flat, ideal for an office if she needed quiet time away from the main house for her research work. She fell in love with the place. The bid went in her favour. Virginia stood aside like a token advisor, silent throughout the proceedings. She checked out all the internal features of the house while Grace strolled around outside. Virginia photographed as much as she could to send to Patience. She asked Virginia to caution Grace on not fully committing to the sale, until she had confirmation that Carlos was indeed coming to Australia. She left Patience to address that matter with her sister.

'I need the change, regardless of what happens, Patience. I feel this is the place I want to be in. If I don't like it, I can always sell, you know. It feels so right, though. I know you are going to say the same when you get here.'

'It's a lot to bear on your own, but if it makes you happy, sis, I won't stand in the way of that? You work so hard.'

'I couldn't take the risk of going in jointly with Keefe just yet. He must prove to me he is well and truly over the alcohol reliance during stressful times. I'm seeing change, I just need reassurance that it's permanent. You know how the slightest trigger can catapult a binge. It's a disease that I cannot have in my personal life.'

'I know he will want stability for Carlos and who better than you to help him with that. He will be the same Keefe you met in Amsterdam, I believe that.'

'Thank you for your optimism as always. You were soft on Keefe from the day he came home to meet you. I do want it to work out, but I should be cautious too. What I feel for him, will not come around again at my age, I am aware of that.'

'So, are you saying you're a geriatric now?' Patience guffawed that Grace had to turn down the volume on her phone to avoid the real estate agent hearing any of their conversation.

Grace told her they were attending Alf's private funeral in Melbourne, although Felicity said they should not rush over, given their heavy schedules.

'We are going to represent you since you are not home yet. What is your expected return date?' Grace could be officious when her guard was up on emotional matters.

'I will be back in a month, I don't intend staying any longer.'

'I hope so.' Grace whispered.

She was open to the changes that had occurred in her life but coming to terms with Patience's frequent trips abroad proved difficult. They both had to move on, the severing of their bond haunted her, a shifting of the axis was in motion to make room for the entrance of newcomers. On the drive home, after she dropped Virginia off at Patience's house, she pondered on her mother's words, *never let a man divide the sisterhood you share.*

Always be there for each other. They teased her about being an advocate for women's rights and that she should consider being a celebrant, she would be creative in the vows she would write. Her wish for them in the later years was that they would look back at their lives and be grateful that they still had each other. Transition was a necessary part of life's journey, and much like the circular arc of a compass, they too would return to their former joys. Varuna's life lessons, her words of wisdom returned often in recent months.

With the property in St Ives secured, Grace packed up the apartment. Virginia told her Lindiwe Johnson was looking for a rental property and wanted to make an offer on her apartment. The real estate agent had the power to choose the most financially viable client. She was tempted to tell the agent to give it to Lindiwe but decided to call Patience for her opinion. Some old habits remained the same between the sisters.

'Don't do it, Grace, let the agent handle it. I am dubious about her.'

Grace knew her sister kept the woman on at the Sisters Helping Sisters Organisation because of Virginia. Lindiwe was still on her payroll. It was never without valid reason that her sister was candid about others, so she accepted the advice and declined a private deal.

Keefe came over for dinner in the middle of the week which they had stopped doing while he was in therapy. He brought a box of assorted cheeses and crackers without his customary bottle of Pinot Noir – he made a concerted effort to avoid alcohol, and that gave Grace some peace of mind. He insisted they start with cheese and crackers first, and a glass of apple juice.

'Dinner is ready, Keefe, let's save this for another day.'

'We have to celebrate, mo'ghra, for the child that is coming to us, your new home and our new beginning.'

They clung to each other on that thought with Grace whispering in agreement, 'We deserve to be happy. I am so proud of your determination to give Carlos a good life, by keeping to your promise to be alcohol-free. You are a good man, Keefe. For that I respect you even more.'

'It is difficult, temptation is all around me. I have noticed that you cleared out the liquor cabinet. Thank you. I'm sorry for shutting you out when all this came at me, and I fell off the wagon... anyone else would have run for the hills. If I'm a good man, you are an even better woman for sticking with me.'

'Who runs away from love?' She wanted to add, 'At my age,' and thought it best to leave it unsaid. That was reserved for her sister's ears, alone.

'Tell me what I want to hear, please tell me you love *me*, Keefe Daly.'

She had always found it difficult to admit how she felt in intimate expressions of love, but this tender moment melted her reserve.

'I love *you*, Keefe, more than you will ever know,' she whispered.

He nuzzled her neck and found her lips for a long and fulfilling commitment to their renewed promise to each other. They remained in still contentment, the dinner Grace prepared was forgotten in the oven as they rediscovered the need they had shut out. Peace settled over them. In the haze of blissfulness Keefe said, 'I want this always, please Grace. When can we be married, mo ghrá?'

'Soon, my love...'

RAIN HAD FALLEN OVERNIGHT and the morning air was heavy with stagnant, humidity. Grace turned to reach for the air conditioner remote control when she realised Keefe was not beside her. She panicked. They were perfect in their joint imperfections, but she dreaded that he might have stepped out for a drink. He was fragile, she needed to know where he was to prevent temptation. The front door opened, and in strolled Keefe with a bouquet of red roses.

'Hey sleepyhead, I have some bakery delights and a piping hot cup of coffee for you. May I bring it in to the bedroom?'

'I thought you ran out on me! No, I have to brush my teeth, first.'

'Never, mo ghrá, that would be like running out on my whole world! Forget brushing your teeth.' He propped her up in the bed and handed her a cup of coffee.

'No, I can't drink this without brushing my teeth! You will be a poor role model for Carlos with this behaviour, Dr Daly!' She laughed and dashed to the bathroom.

'Hurry,' he called after her, 'I need to remind you that you promised to marry me soon. We have a date to set and a wedding to plan.'

'Now I need to shower, splash on perfume, and wear a decent dress before I can discuss those matters,' she teased with a cheeky grin.

He was afraid she might have second thoughts. Could it have been the romantic night together, that seduced her into agreeing they should be married soon? He had to censor his doubt. The balcony was damp after the night's rain, they stayed indoors, chatting, sipping their coffee.

'The florist downstairs was curious when I pounded at the shop door at an unearthly hour!'

'What did you say to her? How embarrassing!' Grace the introvert, the professional woman was not too far beneath the surface.

'I would never say anything to embarrass you, mo ghrá. I told her my lady said yes! That was enough for her to add in a few more roses!'

She shot him a dubious look.

'You sure, you said just that? I don't want her giving me strange looks when I go to the florist.'

'Aye, I swear I did.' He reached over to tickle her for a smile.

They had a restful morning with a bit of wedding talk slipped in before they headed off to work. Grace did not want a big wedding, a small reception with Aileen, Patience and Felicity was enough.

'What about Andrew, surely you'd want to include him, and I'm not sure about Nina, she's had another baby so traveling might be on hold, I think.'

'Certainly, Andrew must be there with us, and leave it to me, I'll contact Nina, it has been a while since we last spoke, she will be excited to know her cupid's arrow hit the mark!' They both recalled the awkward days of their first encounter as two intro-verted medics at the conference in Amsterdam. Their beating hearts were unstoppable after Nina Holstead introduced them.

They were at that stage where nesting was part of the natural cycle of life, and on Saturday morning they flew to Melbourne for Alf's funeral.

As one chapter ends the next begins. Such was the circle of life.

24

REQUEST

Azmil immersed himself in understanding how things were run at the Panna Centre until the shattering call from Pakistan.

Akbar assisted at the Well Study Centre to give Azmil time off to travel to India. Maimoona stepped in to assist him during this time. He knew she had the potential to lead, but he was grooming her for taking over from him. Pakistan left him restless, and in need of change.

He dismissed the students that afternoon and completed some work when he remembered there was a leak in one of the bathrooms. The secrecy of the centre had to be maintained, no workmen could be employed for repair work. Akbar and Azmil took care of everything underground.

WHEN HE FAILED to return by morning, his wife tried calling him with no success. She was afraid to send her daughters out to look for their father, she called Azmil with the news and asked him to notify Masuyo and other Mission members about the situation.

Azmil returned to Pakistan to assist Maa Zenab. He left on the afternoon flight from India. Ojala arranged a prayer meeting with students and staff at the centre, for positive energy for Akbar's safe return. Everyone met him briefly in the week of Akanya's funeral. A tense afternoon followed, waiting for news from Azmil once he had arrived and investigated the situation in Pakistan.

He called Patience late that night, dejected and exhausted.

'Nothing – not a sign of him. It seems he left in a hurry, the centre was not locked, as it usually is. Anyone could have entered after he left. It's not like him to be negligent about such things, in a place like this.'

'Do you think he is in hiding, or is there fear that the rebels might have kidnapped him?'

'It's the latter I'm afraid that seems more like it. He would have informed Maa Zenab if he was going into hiding.'

'Yes, he is a sensible, caring man, that is what I would have thought he'd do.'

'I can file a missing persons' report, but I can guarantee that it will be shelved, because Akbar baba is not a celebrity, or some other big shot they would do anything to protect.'

'Have you called Masuyo, perhaps she could assist?'

'Would you please call her on my behalf, I have not spoken to her before...'

'Yes, certainly. Azmil, please don't go back to the Well Study Centre until we know what's happened to Akbar.'

'I won't, it's dangerous to do so. The students are at the house with Maa Zenab, and I'm staying in the outhouse there. I agree we need to be cautious. Talk again soon.' He hung up leaving Patience terrified that if this was a targeted attack, then, he too was in danger.

Masuyo was devastated to learn that Akbar was missing. As her right-hand person in Asia, he faced danger every day. He was her listening ear and advisor on matters that disturbed her.

'We are thin with the number of men I can send out there to assist Azmil in locating Akbar. I will try to send out two people right away. Keep in close telephone contact. I am grateful that you have stayed on in India. With this situation arising, can you hold the fort there for a while longer. I need you on the Pakistan problem now.'

'I don't think I can commit to that, although I want to ensure that Akbar is safe. There's a lot happening at home, I need to go back to Australia.'

Masuyo was quiet for a few seconds.

'My thinking is to send you to Pakistan to assist Azmil and Maimoona and that Xandria will come over to India to assist Ojala.'

'I really can't go to Pakistan, yet. Are you able to send Xandria sooner so that I might make my exit?'

She did not want to explain why Felicity and Grace needed her as much as India, Pakistan and the Mission.

'I prefer having you oversee Ojala until she can fully take over in Panna, but I understand that family calls have to be answered. I can have Xandria over in India in two weeks.'

'Great!' Patience was overjoyed that within two weeks she would be with Grace and Keefe, and there when Carlos arrived. 'My sister will be grateful, thank you for your understanding, Masuyo. Will Alexis be able to assist in Pakistan?' She knew she might be pushing her luck, but it was worth asking.

'I'm afraid not,' was the terse reply she received, 'a crisis has arisen in the Congo and she has to avail herself for that.'

She felt trapped, wanting to be there beside Azmil, but Grace needed her. Before she opened her mouth to make any voluntary offers of assistance to the Mission, she had to ensure she knew what was expected of her.

'I've been in conversation with Azmil, he says Maimoona is doing a sterling job there. He is distressed with the lack of police involvement, and the need to keep things under wraps on the Well Study Centre location, although the rebels might have this information.'

'Yes, this does not augur well for the centre there. It seems we have to consider shutting it or relocating to another site.'

Closing the centre in Pakistan was a shocking thought. This implied that Akbar was in far more trouble than anybody was prepared to reveal.

Patience spoke to Ojala about Xandria coming over to India to assist her with the centre. This was not well received, she tensed and complained that it was not a good idea.

'She was aloof when she came over for Kanya-ma's funeral. How will she assist if she does not communicate with us?'

She had every right to be concerned. Patience enjoyed seeing this outspoken side of Ojala. It suggested that she had stepped up and was closer to being able to lead than she was a few weeks ago. Fear held back leaders with potential – Ojala was ready to improve her skills to steer the centre. She concurred that Xandria and Alexis were non-communicative while they were in India, for whatever reason. They were locked in their rooms like untouchables.

'Perhaps they were afraid for their own safety, who knows?'

'Then why come to India at all?'

'I know. Don't fret, it's a temporary arrangement. I will keep in touch with you from Australia.'

'How I wish you could stay on, sister Patience.'

'Family matters have come up, and I have to be there to offer my support. Who knows, I might come back to check in on you.'

Ojala was satisfied with that.

DEPUTY INSPECTOR MANIK LAL turned up at the centre. He chatted with Deepak and asked to see Patience.

He said he was on a routine check to ensure they were safe and secure at the centre. Patience told him she was returning to Australia in a fortnight.

'Who will help, Ojala? He asked with concern mapped on his already creviced forehead, and a twitch of his moustache.

'Someone is coming out to assist her.'

'It won't be the same without you,' he whispered. She thought that was what she heard him say.

'Will you return to India?' He said this expecting an immediate answer.

'Perhaps, I'm not sure, yet.'

'You have a family in Australia? Husband? Children?' He slipped in that additional bit of personal investigative questioning with no qualms that Patience might be offended by his prying.

'I have my sister, and her partner and a little boy is soon to arrive in our family. I'm not married. I have not met the right person,' she joked.

His moustache twitched a few times, he narrowed his eyes in disbelief that she had never found love.

'I would like to visit Australia one day. I believe it is a beautiful country.'

'It sure is. You should make a trip there.' She had lost count of how many people she had invited to Australia since she arrived in India. It was time she kept a roster to avoid having them all arrive at the same time!

The sudden change from his previous austere disposition did not prepare her for being awkward in how to respond to his request.

'Before you leave India, would you dine with me at my favourite restaurant?'

His humility, and simplicity were achingly obvious.

'Thank you, that's lovely of you, but are you sure?'

Her intention was not to doubt his invitation to dinner, but she feared her awkward reaction might have offended him. He responded as though she had accepted the invitation.

'Very good! I will arrange it and tell you the day and time. I will send a taxi to collect you.' He raced through the arrange-ments in fear that she might change her mind. He added, 'Any favourite food?'

'Chicken curry!' she laughed, 'I miss the way my sister cooks it for me.'

He nodded, smiling until his round cheeks shone and his tea-stained teeth were visible beneath his scraggly moustache.

'Very good! That is settled! I will see you soon.'

She reached out her hand to shake his, 'Thank you Deputy Inspector.' It felt like the closure to a business transaction.

'Drop the formality,' he said, reaching for her hand, 'Manik, will do.' His abrupt manner was something she grew accustomed to in her appreciation of his humility.

She watched him walk away, sure that she perceived a bounce in his step. He turned around and waved at her, tipping his police cap. A Mr Darcy after all, she smiled.

Hiyana giggled like a thirteen-year-old school girl when Patience told her the Deputy Inspector was taking her to dinner.

'You have a date with the policeman? He must fancy you to return, pretending he is on a routine check for our safety. They never do that here. He came to check on *your* safety, sister!' She fell into the wicker chair doubled with laughter.

'In my experience, Indian men take you to meet their moth-ers, not to a restaurant for a romantic dinner!'

'Stop it, Hiyana. He is a polite gentleman, and we struck up a friendship during the investigation. I told him I was leaving for Australia and he was hospitable enough to invite me to a meal. That's how it is in my country.'

'It certainly is not so here! He wants to impress you, that says a lot about his intentions. I hope he marries you and you stay in India forever!'

'Don' be silly, now. It has nothing to do with marriage, just a friendly dinner.'

'Have you told Ojala yet, that she has nothing to fear, you will be staying after all.' Her chest ached from laughing so much.

'No, that's not true, look at you, you're like a naughty schoolkid!'

'You don't get it, sister, he's serious about you or he won't spend his rupees on you!'

Hiyana left Patience to speculate on the Deputy Inspector's intentions. He presented as polite and respectful or was there a level of truth in what Hiyana said. Maybe she did not really understand the minds of Indian men.

She called Grace to confirm that she would be home in a fortnight, not a month like she had envisaged. Grace was happy about her dinner invitation but issued her sisterly warning.

'Be careful with these uniformed persons, especially police officers, they cannot be trusted, and while you think you're at home there, you are nothing more than a foreigner.'

'I cannot believe you're saying that! It's such a generalisation, and so unlike you. You don't know him, and you've judged him.'

'Now it scares me that you are defensive over him.'

She chose not to respond and told Grace she would email her travel details and see her in two weeks.

PATIENCE SAT on the deck chair outside her room. It was another balmy night, and restlessness left her pensive over Grace's and Hiyana's reactions to her dinner plans with Deputy Inspector Manik Lal. 'Manik, will do' was perhaps the informality she should heed.

25

NEW LIFE

Things moved quickly – Keefe received mail that Carlos could be legally removed from Spain, now that he had full custodial rights. His deep blue eyes sparkled after many weeks, and his smile returned when the letter arrived.

It was a month before they could move into the new home. Too many changes within a short space of time would unsettle Carlos – his mother's death, discovering his papi, and moving to a new country. After much contemplation, Keefe decided that Carlos had to be brought over immediately. He was afraid that Antonio would try to interfere again.

'It's a good idea to get him over ASAP. How about asking Diane to bring him over so that it is beneficial to them both. She will be happy seeing his new home and he won't notice the change as much if she is with him. What do you think?'

'Mo ghrá, you think things through and put Carlos first. That makes me so happy, and Camila would have accepted you as Carlos' new mam.' He reached out to hug her.

'No so fast, Dr Daly, you should ask Diane, first, if she is happy with such an arrangement. She may stay the full three months if she agrees, and if it makes her happy, we can extend her visitor's visa.'

'Aye, you're right. I will have to get onto this quickly.'

Keefe called Aileen, and Grace sent Patience a text message on the latest development on Carlos' move. Both sisters sent their blessings and were glad he might be arriving with Diane. With all that was happening in her life, Grace raised her concern that there was no further news on Akbar's disappearance.

'I'm worried that this is a targeted attack after what happened to Akanya,' Patience said.

Grace trembled, 'I'm glad you're getting away soon. Be careful on that dinner date, now. Seems you and Carlos might be home at the same time.'

'I can't wait to see him and watch him play with Ajax and Sprite,' she squealed.

'Yes, that will be wonderful, good times are on its way!'

KEEFE HAD good news that Diane had accepted the invitation to settle Carlos in Australia. She was not sure if she could stay for the full three months. She lived alone after her mother died, four years ago. Her father had abandoned the family after she was born, she had no one to run her day to day affairs over a long period. Keefe's act of kindness was graciously welcomed. The only time she ever had any authentic people around her was when she and Camila became friends before Carlos' birth. Losing Carlos would be as painful as reliving Camila's death. Now she was invited to be part of his transition into his new life and was promised continued involvement in his future. She had never traveled outside Spain until Keefe gave this opportunity. Through her he gained an understanding of Camila's life and personality. She mirrored for him the type of mother Camila was. He had to keep Camila's memory alive, for Carlos, and requested that Diane bring along as many photographs as she could, of

Carlos with his mother. With everything almost settled, and still lots more to prepare for Carlos' arrival, Keefe decided to have that conversation again with Grace.

'When can we legalise our union, mo ghrá. I want you to be Carlos' mother from the outset?'

'Legalise is a cold word, Dr Daly, but I would be very happy indeed to be your, 'legal' wife and mum to your boy, *our* boy. I would do it today, if I could.'

Keefe stared at her, making sure he understood that she was being earnest.

'Do you mean that?'

'Have you known me to be flippant about something as serious as this?'

That afternoon they sat down at the computer and applied for their marriage registration.

They decided that a celebrant at the house to solemnise the marriage once Patience was back in Sydney, was all they wanted.

'Do you mind going ahead with our plans to be married while Diane is here? I know you prefer it as small as possible with just Aileen, Patience and Andrew, and I'm not sure what Nina has said to you.' Keefe said with a worried look, desperate that Grace should be happy.

'Yes, Diane is welcome, she will be family now. I haven't called Nina, I sent an email and haven't had a reply. If she decides to come with her family, I'm happy with that. I know Felicity might not come, it's too soon for her, but that's where it ends, nobody else, please Keefe.'

In the space of an afternoon, marriage and new parenthood was confirmed by mutually consenting adults who had had a fair share of life's challenges between them and knew this was right. Aileen and Patience wanted to take care of all the arrangements for their siblings. Grace decided she would retain her professional title, as Dr Sharvin with the emotional connection to her father, in his dream for her to be a doctor.

Keefe wanted to celebrate with full acceptance that champagne was out of the question. He called Andrew and Aileen to join them for snacks that evening. Aileen was on her way back from a meeting and would arrive later. Keefe was grateful that Aileen had moved to Sydney after mam's passing, he needed his family around him and treasured her for taking that leap.

Andrew arrived at 6:30 pm with the biggest bunch of red roses he could find. He congratulated them with genuine joy, but Grace caught the longer than usual look he gave her – the finality hit him, something he knew ever since Keefe arrived in Australia. His love was not as changeable as the weather, but he kept his desires hidden, grateful that Grace wanted his friendship. She felt a tinge of sadness for him.

'We have more great news, Carlos will be here soon, and I will officially be his mum. We marry and become parents all in one go! The joys of middle age!' She laughed and hoped he was comfortable with the news they had to share.

'You both deserve the very best. I am so honoured to be part of your joy and celebrations. Remember that Uncle Andrew is always here should you need a babysitter on date nights. Although I suspect I will have to fight both your sisters on that!'

Keefe shook his hand, 'Thank you, Andrew, that means a lot to us. Carlos needs good male role models, Antonio was not the best and I was absent during his early impressionable stage.'

Grace hugged Andrew, he clung to her a little longer, as his reassurance that they were all going to be okay. Aileen arrived to spread her cheer on their good news.

'Look at my two, favourite people, glowing in love. If I should be so lucky!' she chuckled.

They thanked her for her well wishes and large basket of snacks. They all abstained from alcohol to support Keefe to maintain his promise to himself and Grace.

'I have one request, for the reception. May I bake a traditional Irish wedding cake? I know mam would want me to do that.'

Grace was happy to accept but Keefe cautioned Aileen that it was a low-key, very small, private event.

'I will not invite all of Sydney, not to worry! I can't misbehave with two doctors in the house, oh pardon me, three!' She winked at Andrew who was enjoying her friendly banter.

'I'm stepping up as brother to Grace, while Patience is away, so I'm happy to fill you in on the do's and don'ts for Dr Sharvin!' Grace wagged her finger at him in friendly reprimand.

Keefe videoed the evening and sent it off to Patience. He added a message at the end.

'We miss you here, tonight, but are leaving our lives in the hands of our sisters and brother, Andrew. Heaven help him, is all I say!'

Patience received the video and invited, Ojala, Hiyana and Deepak to view it with her, and celebrate over a cup of cardamom tea.

'I can't believe my sister has finally committed to what will be a wonderful union. Bless them both.'

She knew that Andrew, although happy for Grace, would be nursing his own silent sorrow that night.

26

TORN BETWEEN WORLDS

When Xandria arrived at the Panna Centre with an officious attitude, ready to get started in her new role, Ojala and Hiyana had a quiet conversation with Patience.

'We are happy to work with her, if she includes us in the decisions she might make, just as you have done.'

Ojala's usual taciturn manner after her last conversation on the matter, had become quite vocal now.

'Friendliness has been Kanya-ma's way at the centre, and we hope that Xandria upholds this, as this is how we flourish in our work.'

Patience listened, understood and admitted to herself that she could not say with any certainty whether Xandria would comply, she was distant during the training days at the Mission. All she could do was suggest a way around developing a working relationship with her.

'Look, she is coming to lend a helping hand, not to take over the centre. You should reach out to her, as hosts, to make her feel welcome as you did with me. Like you are talking to me now, have this open forum with her. That should alleviate any problems.'

'Thank you, sister. We hope to stay in touch with you, we need your good sense.'

'Certainly, you can call me any time, but I believe you will work out your own solutions to issues. You both have good heads on your shoulders, you better believe that!' Then she added, 'Just don't grow big heads!' Patience's laughter was unsuccessful in removing the early frowns from their young, troubled foreheads.

THINGS GREW tense in Pakistan with no news on Akbar's whereabouts.

Zenab withdrew into spiritual silence. Her husband did everything for her and their daughters. She accepted a quiet, maternal role in their home. Akbar's role in the Mission was his family's priority, they all respected what he did. Her daughters feared she would not return from the pain of her grief, while their father's situation remained a mystery. They were preparing to leave for Australia and needed answers or heaven forbid, closure to the situation. They selected Sydney as the place to keep close to Patience as Akbar suggested. Zenab would not leave Pakistan until she knew what had happened to her husband.

Masuyo's mercurial change of plan for Alexis to go to Pakistan, aggrieved Patience, after she categorically refused to send her to India because of a pressing issue in the Congo. When the Mission faced a risk in the East, she changed her decision with consummate ease.

Azmil communicated their needs through Patience and Masuyo called Patience every day for updates. The young woman from South Africa, almost taken as a concubine by an ageing chief, was significant on the international landscape, between Australia, India and Pakistan. Her life's inspiration impacted on many young women, and older women struggling under harassment, this got her noticed and head-hunted. Alexis' arrived in Pakistan with Judd Knight to assist in Akbar's search, and to set up a new training location. The Well Study Centre, tucked away in an abandoned part of the wheat field, was no longer a safe option. Judd planned to approach the police for assistance under the guise of being a close friend to Akbar. On no account could anything be said about the Mission's activities in Pakistan.

A brief trip to Pakistan was necessary for Patience to get Zenab to communicate with Judd. He needed information on Akbar's personal life to help him to pull off a believable representation as a concerned close friend.

Zenab had remained locked in her bedroom and assumed the customary mourning of wives in being cloistered for four lunar months. Contact with men was to be avoided. Patience was the only person other than her daughters, allowed into her room. She tried to persuade Zenab not to give up hope as no evidence suggested that Akbar was dead. Although she spent a few months in Pakistan when she was assigned to the Well Study Centre, this was the first time Zenab held a conversation with her.

'This is like a death to me, sister. Not seeing him every day, or hearing his voice and jokes has left me empty, just not knowing...'

Patience understood loss, her father, mother, Petros and Mama Varuna left her sad for a long time, but she had to summon the strength to go on. It was harder for Zenab who had spent many years with Akbar, she had no other family apart from her two daughters who gave her every reason to live. Sometimes certainty of death paved a way for coming to terms with the finality of life, not knowing conjured untold visions of what might have happened to Akbar.

'I understand, Maa Zenab, but only you can help us get closer to the truth on what happened. You must speak to Judd to give him information that he can use to get the police on our side. Although, I am loathed to admit it, we need their assistance with the search.'

After several hours of deliberation, Zenab conceded that he was the only hope of getting closer to what happened on the day

Akbar disappeared. She placed Patience in an awkward predicament when she asked, 'Can you stay with me until my husband is found. I feel calm around you.'

The request wrenched Patience's heart – she had great difficulty in refusing a part of herself to those in need. She had to tell Zenab it was not possible. It was important that she returned home to be present for her sister's needs.

Zenab accepted and understood that there were times when family had to be first on a long list of demands.

'You have to be there for your sister. She needs you. It's an important time in her life and your mothers are not here anymore. You will come back once the child is settled, right?'

'Without a doubt, if you still need me then, I will. You should come to Sydney with Azmil and your daughters, it was Akbar sir's wish, you know.'

Zenab was silent – she shook her head dismissing the suggestion.

'I cannot leave until I know... either way... I won't be at peace...'

Patience let it be. Zenab was close to a break down. They both knew that so many days with no word meant one of two things, Akbar was in a torture camp for his association with the Mission, or dead.

With only three days in Pakistan, Patience hoped to bring some peace to Azmil too. He was awkward with strangers and needed to be led into working with Judd and Alexis. She told Alexis that Zenab needed the emotional and cultural space now to preserve her sanity.

It felt strange articulating TUC virtues to Alexis who directed the values during their training at the Mission. Alexis was a leader with an aloofness that made her insensitive – the uniqueness of culture had to be understood to avoid unwittingly injuring a fragile soul.

Azmil asked if she could extend her stay but also accepted that family matters needed her attention.

'I am grateful for your support and know you will be a telephone call away.'

'You have an inner strength you have not seen in yourself. Maa Zenab needs you. Trust that and act, accordingly, let instinct guide you.'

'It is what I want. To bring stability back for Maa Zenab and her daughters is what I hope to achieve. This is what she gave me as a lost waif when she warmly welcomed me as a child from the dust. I fear that Akbar baba will not return, time is running out on hope.'

'Never turn your back on hope, never. Leave it to Judd and the police now, but we have to hope,' she said with deliberate softness.

JUDD MADE his first visit to the police in Karachi. Armed with photographs of himself photoshopped in as a long-standing friend of Akbar's. He sat across the desk from the Assistant Inspector General of Police, aware of corruption scandals and loads of misdemeanours created by a lack of justice for victims. All preconceived notions had to be thrown out if he hoped to win the inspector's trust and respect.

'You are American?' The inspector asked in a raised voice, posing the question with obvious suspicion.

'I am sir, but Akbar was a brother to me hence my keenness to find him.'

'I see. Was he a business associate, with his wheat business?'

'No, sir, we are friends.'

The Assistant Inspector General's cold eyes, and body language indicated that Judd was not trusted.

'I see. How did you meet? When did you meet? Where did you meet?'

His tone was aggressive.

'We met at a human rights conference in New York about fifteen years ago.

The inspector raised his eyebrows.

'I see, you share political views.'

His repetitive use of 'I see,' prefacing every comment he made, left Judd thinking that what he expected to achieve might not occur. He seemed to have taken Judd's skull, opened it up, and picked up what he deemed a truth and a lie.

It was an exhausting afternoon repeating everything he had to say while being careful that each thing he uttered was in sync with what he said before. The devilled dilemma of maintaining a lie was important to win the support needed to find Akbar.

Finally, the Assistant Inspector General agreed that he would put two men on the case. His passing comment as Judd stood up to thank him and leave, echoed with the realisation that the inspector knew everything he needed to know on Akbar's case.

'Yes, your friend, I remember now, adopted a child. A boy whose mother was a young Pakistani woman who had an illegitimate child with an American airman. Yes, I remember him... Who can forget that?'

Judd shook the inspector's hand and left.

The inspector was kind enough to see him but left the perception that nothing would be done to find Akbar. Judd had to rethink his strategy.

He debriefed with Alexis, telling her she should accompany him on the next visit to the inspector, as his wife. His reasoning was that it would add credibility that Akbar was indeed a family friend.

Patience detested deception. She wanted a perfect world, but perfection was an illusion when dealing with rogue police and politicians for whom cunning manipulation was a way of life.

She had one day left in Pakistan and set aside time to meet with Maimoona. She was a busy lady, managing the school that was now run from Akbar's home, and ensuring that the students remained safe.

The same startlingly light brown eyes, as if the switch had been turned on at the back of her head, met Patience in a moment of familiarity. Yet they had encountered each other, once only, at the orphanage in Karachi. Her former, restless pacing, and biting comments on the liars that visited the orphanage with false promises, now exhibited a stillness and maturity beyond her years. Her intensity was the same, but she glided across to Patience in surreal serenity.

'Sister Patience, welcome, lovely to see you again. Mashallah, you look well, just as I remember you.'

'My goodness look at you. I left, and you became a woman. I am so happy to see you, and more especially, to see you here!' Patience enclosed Maimoona's hands in hers – her African demonstration of respect.

'Leadership and responsibility ensure that a speedy growing up occurs.' She laughed, and her eyes grew lighter.

'You kept your word, sister, you did not come back, but you made sure I was remembered, hence I'm here.'

She explained that she was grateful for Alexis' assistance. This brought tremendous relief and freedom from guilt to Patience who was departing from Pakistan, on the early morning flight, the next day. She felt a sisterly connection when Maimoona said, 'Meeting Akbar sir after you left was like reuniting with my father. Being here has brought me immense peace for which I thank you.'

'There is not a person, I believe, who will say any less of Akbar, he has been wonderful to me too.'

She was comforted that the Pakistan centre was in good hands. It would be marvellous, in time to come, to have Maimoona visit Australia, to motivate abused women at the SHSO safe houses. This would prove, what she upheld, that in angst and joy all are indeed one under a common sky of humanity.

It was time to return to her SHSO although Virginia was doing an excellent job in keeping the sisters safe from harm. Her first project would always tug at her like a firstborn child. She wanted to be back there, assisting Virginia.

Patience left her soul in many places, dispersed by duty, but she knew her arrivals and departures were temporary. She would return time and time again when she was needed.

27

SONGS OF HOME

Patience arrived in Sydney, relieved to be back on familiar terrain, yet the call of India was under her skin, a constant reminder that she had left unfinished business.

A cool morning lightened her step after endless hot days in Panna, and nights of stolen sleep that left her restive, listening to the raspy whirring of the ceiling fan, but strangely refreshed the next morning.

Carlos was arriving in two days with Diane, and she wanted to be there to welcome the newcomers to their family. She expected Grace to be anxious with the child arriving, preparing for a new home and committing fully to her relationship with Keefe.

She caught a cab from the airport and asked the driver to stop at her home first for a catch up with Ajax and Sprite before she headed to see Grace. Her dog-babies were lovingly loyal, they clambered for her affection, pressing themselves against her, whimpering like neglected children one minute, then dancing around in a wild attempt to be noticed. She hugged them close, 'I'm here, boys, mama's home to spoil you, for a while...'

After two hours of shared love, she showered and drove over

to Grace's apartment. The visitor's parking spot allocated to Grace, still bore the sign, 'Reserved for Patience.' She smiled thinking there were so many ways that could be interpreted – a sort of spiritual reminder. The underground parking lot brought back many memories of Grace's anxiety of being alone in that space. This was their first home in Sydney after spending two years in the country. Grace was living out of boxes, now, in preparation for the big move to the new house, in a few weeks. Changes were apace, the inevitability of life, that had to be accepted along with whatever else arrived.

Grace clung to Patience with the same fervour as Sprite and Ajax did just a few hours earlier. She had a feast prepared, like a doting mother, to welcome her sister back. Virginia was to join them for lunch.

'So how are you and Keefe doing, you must be bubbling in anticipation of Carlos' arrival?'

'We are. Keefe is in a much better space now that everything is out in the open. He's not one to harbour secrets and feels free now, and for that I love him more!'

Patience saw the transition from the tension between Keefe and Grace when she left for India, to this newfound gratitude and love. It was never easy for Grace to express her feelings to others, apart from her mother and Patience. They were raised as sisters by different mothers where truth was the binding force. The Mission's first value was truth, and to witness Grace celebrating its value in her love for Keefe was special for Patience.

'To see you glow, makes this a happier homecoming. I couldn't be more excited for you both.'

'Thank you. It's wonderful that you and Aileen are going to be important people in Carlos' life.

Patience, true to form, seized the opportunity for some sisterly mirth.

'So, who's more special, Aileen or me? Who will be the godparent? I'm a big girl, I can take it, just don't disappoint me!'

She laughed her caramel husky laugh which poured in warmth over Grace.

'It's a role you will share.'

'Not good enough, Dr Sharvin! I say leave it up to Carlos to decide who will be his favourite aunt!' she giggled, amused by how quickly she and Grace slipped into being children again. Grace prodded Patience for information on how long she was going to stay in Australia and whether she would return to India.

'I'm here for family matters and to assist Virginia with the SHSO but will be on call to the Mission if issues need my attention. So, no plans to return to India or Pakistan on the cards for me.'

'I hope so, Patience,' is all Grace said.

Virginia arrived at 1 pm with dessert and a box of chocolates.

'It seems we never leave, and you are always returning from an assignment, more experienced and wiser from your travels.'

'Soon you'll be doing the same. Now, these chocolates are not what the doctor ordered, so we shall have to share them.'

Virginia bubbled with excitement that everything was going to plan for her wedding. It was to be a small affair and she wanted Grace and Patience to be her bridesmaids.

'We are too old to be bridesmaids,' Grace groaned, 'don't you have younger friends or cousins? I don't want to be mutton dressed like lamb!'

'No cousins, I would so love you both to be my bridesmaids,' she implored, 'you raised me from my empty life and directed my new path.'

'Tell us what you need done, and if you are happy with a pair of golden girls, then we are it!' Patience said this, nodding for acknowledgement from Grace who did not look at all pleased at the thought of being a bridesmaid.

The afternoon passed in friendly conversation that helped to temporarily lift weighty thoughts of Akbar and his family, and the people she left behind to fend for themselves. Virginia returned to the office and Patience promised to come in the next day. Before Keefe arrived, the conversation took on an earnest intensity.

'How did your date with the police officer go?'

'Manik Lal? It wasn't a date! Just a friendly gesture from a nice guy.'

'You believe that's all it was?'

'Yes.'

'Has he been in touch with you after you left India?'

'No, and that is my point, he has no reason to be in touch with me.'

'I'll leave it alone, but something tells me he's sweet on you. Now that Virginia is settling down, and Keefe and I are tying the knot, where do you see yourself in forming a permanent relationship with this guy?'

'Oooh, this is serious, Grace. I feel it's an inquisition with my Mamas!'

'Well, what do you say?'

'I don't know, really, it's not uppermost in my mind. You are the lucky one with two dashing fellas vying for your attention. I have no romantic thoughts, and heaven forbid I have no feelings for Manik. Drop it, sis!'

'I need to know you have intentions of being settled soon, get serious now.'

'I don't know. Work is my life, and nobody has stolen my heart.'

Grace paused with a look of concern.

'I want you to find love, I know you will when the time is right, but you have to be open to the possibility. I will get Keefe involved to introduce you to one of his colleagues, if this Manik fellow has not made your pulse race.' Grace was as serious as a Victorian mother proposing a business deal to secure her daughter a husband. Patience heard her own voice in Grace's words of encouragement, with an extra dash of urgency that she finds a partner right now!

'A doctor? No thank you! Are you kidding me? What's with you these days with wanting to marry me off?'

Keefe arrived an hour earlier than expected, putting an end to their speculations and choices on men. Only two women who were as close as they were, could open their hearts to such matters. Keefe looked thinner since she last saw him. His blue eyes were brighter in his somewhat smaller face. The thick rush of red hair was beginning to thin at the front. Too soon, she thought, this ageing was happening too soon. His spirit was warm and caring as ever.

'Hey, Patience, so good to have you back!'

Grace knew that Keefe was happy that Patience was around to lift the responsibility off him when she was in a fragile state. He loved her with ardour, but her idiosyncrasies, fears and compulsions collided with his laid-back attitude. She had to be busy all the time. He loved lolling in front of the television on his days off. She warned him that fatherhood demanded being present in every moment, and that his lounging around would soon be history. When Patience asked him how he was feeling about Carlos' arrival, his face lit up, his cheeks filled out with a broad smile. She saw the twinkle in his eye.

'What do you think? I'm elated, I tell you. Aye, and Grace is bursting more than I am, she's bought a new house and everything,' he laughed.

'That's true, I can't wait!' Grace cooed.

'That's one lucky boy coming to the Sharvin-Daly home. I'm so happy for you both!' Patience slapped Keefe on the arm.

'One lucky dad here to have the blessing of knowing about my son and to be able to raise him with your sister. What's the chances of that happening if his poor mum was not ill? Life...' he stopped and looked away.

Patience left after her chat with Keefe, to give her sister time and space to plan all the final details for Carlos' arrival. She went to bed, had a look at her phone, many text messages waited for her attention. One from Ojala and Hiyana who were keen to know if she was safely at home and enjoying being with her sister. She replied, *All's well. Thank you for asking. Will be in touch soon. Take care, Patience x.'*

The message that left her drained of her last ounce of energy was from Azmil.

The brevity said much.

The police have abandoned the search for Akbar baba. Deeply saddened.

Patience tossed around typing and erasing messages, unsure of the best way to say what needed to be said without disappointing Azmil. Finally, a short message, *Never, give up, I'll call you tomorrow.*

CARLOS FLORES ARRIVED on a 10 am flight from Spain with the devoted Diane. Felicity called to let Grace know she planned to be in Sydney soon, to meet Carlos. Grace mulled over why she felt the urgency to do this when she was still mourning Alf's passing. She simply said, 'I want your boy to know me, as an aunt, a friend of the family, whatever! As someone who cares about you, Keefe and Patience. He must know me.' Grace knew from experience that going against Felicity's wishes was not ideal, she had to accept that curiosity or a genuine need to support her might be the motivation. She let it go understanding that loneliness triggered this reaction. Felicity's desperation to be included saddened her.

They drove to the airport laden with a large teddy, little presents wrapped like it was Christmas again, and a box of lollies that might not be too good for a growing boy's teeth! At the airport, Grace grabbed a large helium balloon that read, 'Welcome Home,' and a bunch of pink roses for Diane. They were excessive, not knowing what was enough, or too much. They had a lot to learn in the parenting department!

Diane's searching eyes looked for Keefe in the crowd. Her plain cream dress, flat nude pumps, and a tan handbag gave her a school-teacher look. She clung to Carlos' left hand, like an anxious mother who was afraid her child would get lost in the crowd. Carlos stood up on tippy-toes looking for Keefe. Diane bent over and whispered in his ear. He let go of her hand, making a dash towards Keefe, calling out, *Papi! Papi!* Grace stood aside and observed, with great surprise, Carlos' excitement upon seeing Keefe. Diane called out behind him, 'Speak English, Carlo.' She lovingly left out the 's' in Carlos' name, just as Camila did.

Keefe grabbed Carlos up into his arms. Grace saw him tremble as he sobbed, tears streamed unabashedly down his reddening face. In that moment she knew Keefe would be okay, he had every reason to feel whole, and free of guilt after the first news he received that he had a child in Spain. He slipped away lost in remorse, but he was back, the gentle, loving Keefe, she met in Amsterdam, was back! Diane stood aside, alone, teary at the sight of the gushing reunion between father and son. Grace walked up to her and introduced herself.

'I'm Grace, welcome to Australia.' Her voice was soft, her eyes searching.

'Thank you. I remember you from the photographs Keefe sent to me. I know Carlos will be well taken care of, thank you for accepting him with open arms.'

Grace knew that this had been a painful time for Diane, bringing Carlos to his father was also severing her bond, in a way, as the only other significant person in this little lad's life. She drew Grace towards Carlos.

'Carlo, this is Grace, you remember from the photographs?'

Carlos leaned forward to be put down on the ground and turned to Grace. He put his little arms around her legs and whispered, *Grace*, he smiled up at her and stretched his arms up to be carried. Grace was overcome with a rush of emotions when he said her name. She sucked in a deep breath, picked him up, and hugged the little, red-haired boy, a replica of Keefe, close to her chest. Diane had reminded him to be loving and polite, she was relieved that he was. All three adults were awash with joy that Carlos had made a positive entrance into Australia into the lives of his new parents.

On the drive to Grace's apartment, Diane said that Carlos' English had improved. There might be the odd word here and there that he was yet to learn. Grace added that they had been brushing up on their basic understanding of Spanish.

'Thankfully you will be around to help us,' Grace smiled at Diane.

'Thank you for inviting me to come over with Carlo. I would have been a nervous wreck sending him alone on that flight.'

'Consider this a home away from home, Diane,' Keefe said.

'Muchas gracias, Keefe.'

'Hah! Speak English, please!' Carlos shouted, pointing a cheeky finger at Diane.

They had a hearty laugh with Carlos joining in on the merriment.

'That's getting my own medicine back,' Diane said, 'I have been drilling him with that line!'

Patience tidied up Grace's apartment and had pancakes ready for Carlos. Diane had told Keefe they were his favourite. Carlos clammed up when he saw Patience, he clung to Diane, burying his head in her shoulder.

Patience whispered to Grace, 'It must be all too much for him meeting strangers in a new place.'

'Aye, he'll settle soon, he was so jolly at the airport, and besides he must be exhausted, poor little man.' Keefe said in lowered tones.

Diane slipped into Spanish to comfort Carlos, telling him

Patience was Grace's sister. He picked up his head, looked at Grace and then Patience.

'Don't worry, darling, there's time yet to get to know each other. You must meet Ajax and Sprite, my dogs, soon. You'll love them.'

Carlos burst into tears, 'No, no, no...'

The gut-wrenching cry of a little lad who recently lost his mother, now in a foreign country after many hours of air travel, thrown amongst new people, reverberated with, *quiero a mi Mamá!*

28

EMBRACING CHANGE

News arrived that Anton Wessels would be in Sydney in a month.

Much was going on with Grace's house move, settling Carlos, and assisting with Virginia's garden wedding in a week, the same week as her house move! She reminded herself to breathe deeply, to limit the number of coffees she consumed to ensure she was not jittery. Andrew persuaded her to take a few days off to get herself organised for the move. He knew she would have collapsed in a heap if she tried to carry all her shifts at ER – working nights and not sleeping during the day with all that was heaped on her platter of life events. Patience took on some of the house move requirements by transporting a few precious items that they feared the removalists might damage during transportation. Varuna's fine crockery was treated with great care, it was the palpable memory of the delectable meals she cooked and served them with love and delight.

With the blinds and curtains fitted, Grace had peace of mind that the house was secure from unsavoury outsiders. After extensive counseling with Dr Deakin to overcome her anxiety and recurring dreams, she still carried the fear of being attacked in some abandoned car park, or that her house on the street was easy access to the outside world. With Patience being bombarded by the media on her front lawn, she was reminded that privacy was easily stolen. Her apartment offered her the security she needed. She had to ensure that her anxiety did not unsettle Carlos. His English proficiency grew by the day, he asked lots of questions. His curiosity was a clear indication of his intelligence in the type of questions he asked. Some moved beyond the concrete to pondering why Grace did her grocery shopping late at night. He enjoyed visits to the supermarket with Camila and asked where the food came from when he had a new tasty breakfast cereal in the morning. She explained that she shopped at night when it was not busy. To her surprise he asked if she did not like people. With a child in the house, she was aware that every move she made in the small apartment was closely observed. A little psychologist questioned her actions, making her contemplate how she presented to him.

Once the initial hurdle of everything happening at the same time was over, there would be room for warm family gatherings in her new home. Diane had Carlos in a routine with plenty play activities to distract him from the upheaval with the wedding plans. He spent many hours with her at the local park, making friends quickly with children who visited the park with their parents or guardians. She was concerned that he would react when he realised that he would not see his little friends as regularly, after they had moved from the neighbourhood. Diane was a godsend during this time, assisting Grace and Patience whenever she could. She was sensitive to their need for private time and strategically took Carlos out to give them space.

Anton's imminent visit made them nostalgic. He was going to be in Sydney for a week. They had to plan the week so that he did not miss out on the lovely sights and sounds of the city.

'He's adamant that he will stay at a hotel, saying he does not want to disrupt my routine.' Grace said.

'Yeah, he was always a considerate man. He can stay at my place. Virginia's moved out, there's plenty space and I'm out most of the day, and some nights anyway. It would probably feel like being at a hotel!' Patience laughed. 'Tell him we won't accept any other arrangement, I think you will be pleasantly surprised that he will accept the offer once you tell him what I said.'

'Yeah, that might be an idea. I will suggest it to him. Are you sure about this?'

'Am I ever not sure, sis?' She pummeled Grace on the arm like a playful puppy.

'You're the one with the common sense I badly lack.'

Keefe had no idea how to manage the domestic front, it was beyond him with a house move, Virginia's wedding, and Carlos arriving. He took to the couch, turned on the telly and extolled how wonderful he thought Grace was, thinking that was enough to let him off the hook. She ensured that he took Diane out and about during the weekend to do the tourist visits that she could not fit into her hectic schedule.

In the flurry of her world, Grace worried if Anton would be comfortable seeing them after all these years. He was close to her mother, but awkward around her.

'I was not very welcoming to Anton, back in the day, in the old country, remember? I'm ashamed to admit I was a little snooty.'

'Oh, I remember! A 'little' snooty, you say?' Patience laughed with the pleasure of seeing her sister squirm. You hated his khaki shorts, and knee-high socks! Poor guy, he was head over heels in love with you, and you broke his heart!'

'Don't exaggerate! I did not break his heart! We barely spoke to each other. He was not head over heels in love at all, maybe a tad smitten, I don't know!'

'Deeply smitten! Anyway, it's great that he's making a trip here to see us. We have to be nice, Gracie.'

'We're older with enough life experience between us, lord knows, so all will be well. I'm hoping we can ask him more about dad's death and if there was ever any further news on the case.'

'Mmm, do you really want to dive back into the past? It could trigger the fear you carried before you knew Boetie Arendse was dead.'

'I am stronger, Patience. I want to know the truth, Mum sheltered me to some extent from knowing the awful truth about Dad's death. I need closure on that and what better person than Anton to bring me, or us through that.'

A hug was all that was needed to accept that they had grown in acceptance of where their lives were at, and where they were headed. As Patience was about to leave for the SHSO office, Carlos burst into the room with Diane trying to restrain him from disturbing them.

'I want to see Ajax and Sprite.' He grabbed Patience from behind, completely over his initial fear of meeting her. Grace was grateful for his resilience, it meant everything to her to have Carlos show affection for her sister. She was the easiest person to love. After his first visit to Ajax and Sprite, with Patience allowing him complete freedom in her home, they were mates for life. She rolled on the carpet with him and the dogs like any child would. He refused to call her 'Aunty Patience,' preferring 'Patience' in his Spanish accent. Each time she heard him call out to her, *Paciencia*, it was music to her ears. Soon Grace was doing the same, whenever she referred to Patience in conversation with Carlos. Slowly but surely positive changes centred their lives, but it was a short-lived joy for her intention at the SHSO office that afternoon.

Virginia had informed her that Lindiwe Johnson was brusque with one of their sponsors, a generous businessman from Melbourne. He said nothing, but Virginia was embarrassed by Lindiwe's rudeness, and mentioned it to Patience. She was more than fair with Lindiwe, but as even-tempered as she was, she was at the end of her tether with this newcomer at SHSO. Patience was a great conversationalist, she enjoyed a joke or two, but the tongue, when it became an overused muscle, had to be warned and dismissed. Talking out of turn to people who are kind was not to be tolerated in her conduct rule book. It was time to have another meeting with Lindiwe.

'You are probably wondering why I have called a meeting with you, today.'

'Yes, I am not sure why, but eager to know.'

'I am sorry to advise that SHSO is no longer in need of a receptionist. I am back and intend to be present here every day for the full duration of the work day, and more.'

'I see,' was all Lindiwe said, as the full intent of Patience's officious words hit her.

'You are a skilled worker and will secure another position soon. I am letting you go, today, directly after this meeting. You will be advanced three month's pay to allow you time to find another job to your suitability.' She reached over and handed Lindiwe her notice of termination with a cheque for three month's advance pay.

She fixed her stony eyes on Patience, 'Is Virginia being asked to leave too?'

'No, she is a co-director in this organisation. We will be running this operation together.'

Without warning, Lindiwe slipped into a tirade in Zulu, ending with, 'Never forget who you are, and where you come from? I am leaving now. I will be out of here in ten minutes. Are you going to watch me clear my desk?'

'That will not be necessary, you can show yourself out.' She stood up and extended her hand, I wish you well.'

Lindiwe backed away and walked out without a word.

Patience was relieved that the ordeal was over. It was the hardest thing she had to do, yet it was the right thing. Lindiwe was hurting the organisation that she had painstakingly set up as a one-woman team working well into the night for several years, building a reputation, and garnering the support of reputable businesses to set up safe houses around the country. Feeling emotionally depleted from the meeting, she had to remind herself that she lived in her truth and had shown compassion and understanding, by allowing Lindiwe to stay on after her first transgression – truth must take precedence. The survival of the SHSO depended on it.

Virginia was relieved that Lindiwe was out for good and surprised that she did not stop to say goodbye.

'You only know what a person's true thoughts are, I suppose, when they are in trouble.'

'I don't agree. The signs were there, that she was flippant about how she conducted herself. We will in due course employ someone else. I will hand it to an employment agency and we both will conduct the final interview to decide the candidate's suitability. As of today, all letterheads will include you as the co-director of this organisation.'

'Thank you, Patience, you are most generous. I will ensure you never regret it.'

'I know, you have already, more than once, proved how valuable you are to me, and Grace.'

They got back to business that day with a celebratory coffee and determination that no sister would be left destitute from poverty or abuse. Grace agreed that it was the right decision to terminate Lindiwe's position.

'It cut when she told me not to forget who I am and where I came from. It felt like a curse was dumped on my head.'

'Rubbish, she's just a disgruntled woman who brought her baggage with her. It's got nothing to do with culture or who you are. I think that's it, you won't hear from her again.'

'I hope so, Grace. It was a tough call today.'

'But, the right one! Good news, Anton has accepted your offer of accommodation while he is in Sydney.'

With the edginess of the day, wedding bells harkened joy with Virginia's and Grace's impending nuptials, and the excitement around Anton's arrival.

29

FURTHER AFIELD

The rapid change of activities, decisions and new beginnings brought joy and peace to Grace. Patience kept her conversations with Azmil private to avoid disturbing the celebratory air of the upcoming joyous unions.

Pakistan was in a deadlock.

The Well Study Centre was still, the voices dimmed as the passion for teaching and learning evaporated in fear for what the future held. Maa Zenab was taken in for questioning. Her daughters were tense and anxious, and Azmil was as helpless as a newborn baby.

Akbar was gone.

Not a trace.

Nobody had any inkling where to begin.

Patience heard the tears in Azmil's voice when he revealed that Maa Zenab was a suspect in Akbar's disappearance. The ludicrousness of the suspicion reeked of political play. It left Patience considering whether the police had unearthed the work the Mission was doing there.

Judd and Alexis appealed to the Chief of Police to see the idiocy of the arrest, claiming that Maa Zenab was a devoted mother and wife. The safety of her daughters was compromised, trapping them indoors when everyone outside was a potential enemy. Azmil feared that Maa Zenab would fall ill from the stress of the arrest. He was traumatised from his visit to the jail. Jeering inmates called out on sight of him, 'Awara Kutta,' leaving him as vulnerable as the little boy who was bullied for his mixed heritage. Maa Zenab, he said, was considered a suspect because she reported her husband missing the following evening. The house was ransacked, and all literature taken. Akbar's framed poems were removed from the house. Allegiance to the organisation was the only reason Maa Zenab held off reporting, right away, that Akbar was missing. They were locked in faithfulness to their marriage, spirituality and the Mission's ideals.

Masuyo was working with a legal team to release Maa Zenab. She asked Judd and Alexis to unearth as much as they could on her character, to disprove police perception of her. Patience's quiet late-night conversations with Felicity had her working through her contacts at The Hague. This saddened her when she thought about scores of people who did not have access to influential others to set them free from erroneous judgements – asylum seekers who were lost at sea, or victims of scams that promised a passage to freedom. She had to impress upon Felicity that nothing could be said about the Mission.

'There's one thing you have to accept is that some knowledge of their existence has slipped out to the wider world when recruits who left the Mission were interviewed on CNN, and A Current Affair, before you returned.'

'It's not for the exclusive protection of the Mission, per se, as it is for the protection of those who are vulnerable in this situation.'

'I know, I will proceed with absolute caution, trust me.'

She wanted to accept this as Felicity's promised truth, but memory returned on her brazen call to Grace's therapist when she perceived that Grace had had a breakdown in Melbourne. Her well meaning friendship, and enthusiasm to set things right, as she perceived it, crossed boundaries that Patience and Grace tolerated. She gave her friend the opportunity to change this perception, only because she seemed to have mellowed after Alf's passing.

Akbar had to be found. The family needed closure and Maa Zenab's name had to be cleared. The organisation's secrecy policy was secondary to restoring a broken family, grieving under the weight of not knowing.

Maimoona was bold. Nothing could deter the care and protection she gave all the young women in her charge. While Azmil could no longer hold back his emotions, the light behind her brown eyes was fierce as she prepared to confront the police on their unfair and unfounded arrest of Maa Zenab. She had the ability to bring any stubborn Superintendent Chief Inspector to his knees. Hardship toughened her. If something or someone mattered to her, she would put her life on the line. Azmil was uneasy with the force she demonstrated and sought Patience's advice on whether she should present a deputation in defence of Maa Zenab.

'Let her go, the more noise we make, the more likely they are to respond. The Hague will get involved too.'

Patience drowned herself in work to avoid the pull she felt to return to Pakistan during this time of crisis in Akbar's family. She had to be there for Virginia and Grace.

Three days later, Maa Zenab was released. Azmil was surprised to see the fire with which she returned. Something he had never seen in her. She contacted Masuyo giving her allegiance to the Mission. She was welcomed with open arms and advised to tell her truth in a personal testimony session. Maimoona recorded the session and sent an encrypted audio file to Patience.

With a palpitating heart, she plugged in her headphones to listen with respectful privacy to Maa Zenab's bravery in sharing her story.

I was born the daughter of an Indian prince and had boundless luxury and pampering from ladies-in-waiting, and food and clothes that I wanted but did not need. It was only when I ventured outside the palace walls that I saw poverty and starvation. I would ask my father to provide food to those who were starving. I stopped eating when he sniggered saying you cannot feed dogs the food of the gods. This was when I came to know who my father really was, a selfish person who would not share the excess he had. The corruptive influence of power is what I learned early in life.

I remember one day, as clear as if it happened yesterday. A mob descended on the palace when a servant was whipped and died from his injuries. His crime was taking an extra serving of rice at dinner.

I could not bear to live within the palace walls any longer. I escaped one night, through the bedroom window, dressed in my lady-in-waiting's uniform, while she slept. I arrived in Pakistan and sought refuge in the orphanage. They had no idea I was from India. I was fluent in Urdu and Hindi, that was my salvation. This was my home until I turned sixteen. I began working that year for a local tailor and assisted with the children at the orphanage, in return for ongoing lodgings at a low rental fee. I felt free and normal, above all I was independent.

One day a dashing young man came in to get his university graduation suit cut and stitched. The tailor took his measurements and I wrote down his requirements. Later, the young man approached me and told me his name was Akbar.

My heart was never still again. His respectful manner was something I had not expected. Palace life did not engender respect for women. My mother remained cloistered in the palace. Years later when I told Akbar, he said it reminded him of Jane Eyre with Rochester's wife locked away. He told me so many meaningful stories and explained why women had to be respected. After several suit fittings he made many excuses that the stitch or cut was not right just so that he could see me again. He invited me to his graduation and my boss gave me the time off to attend. His wife sewed me a beautiful dress. They had no children and took great delight in seeing my love story unfold. My husband's intention became clear when he introduced me to his peers, at the graduation, as his 'wife to be.' That very afternoon he proposed, and I accepted. A month later we married. Soon he asked me to give up work at the tailor to start my own business from home. He worked very hard at the university and I sewed women's outfits. The tailor and his wife became godparents to my daughters. They both have since passed on. It was after my eldest daughter's birth that I revealed who I really was to my husband. He said, 'You were a princess from the day I set eyes on you.'

After he left his job at the university, and by this time Azmil was our son – the brilliant light that had entered our lives, it was then that my husband took on working with the Mission. We lived a nomadic life until I told him, after the birth of our second daughter, that we needed a secure home base to raise the children. He purchased the wheat farm and the rest is history as you know. When women had no voice, my husband sought advice from me, and listened to my needs. He committed to raising the bar of respect for women.

No matter the outcome, we must fulfil what he set out to do. He passed on the leadership to you. Wherever he is, I pray he is at peace and appeal for your prayers for him. Thank you.

AZMIL THANKED everyone for their time and attention and announced that he had written a tribute poem to his Maa and Baba. He read it out in a heavy, steady voice.

Two Lives, One Life
Left in the Wilderness
Alone in this Life

Ray of sunlight
Light of Hope
Beacon of Compassion
My Father you came to me
My Mother you took me in

Made me yours
Out of the dust of life
You picked me up
Whispering, I see you

Two lives, one Life
Two Countries, One Child
Out of the Wilderness
Into Family life

Courage, Love, Conviction
You Gave Me Life
I salute you

PATIENCE REPLAYED the recording a few times, moved by Azmil's poem as a mirror of her own life with the Sharvin family, and for the truth on Zenab's life.

The Well Study Centre operated from Akbar's home with Maa Zenab and Maimoona heading the centre. Azmil retreated into the world of poetry writing and researching his ancestry.

He kept Akbar's memory alive.

30

ENTWINED

Virginia's wedding on Saturday afternoon created a ripple of excitement.

Felicity arrived three days earlier to assist in whatever way she could. Grace was pleased to see that Felicity had finally given Virginia the attention and respect she deserved. Grace moved into her new home with Keefe, Diane and Carlos on Friday morning. She was frazzled with the wedding coming up the next day. Dr Deakin's words returned to remind her that not everything in life had to be perfect, except for doctors who had to be accurate to save lives. Even then there were always issues that crept in, testing their capacity to have control over life and death. In some ways Grace felt like the mother of the bride, saving Virginia from the mistakes she had made in her life. Patience stepped in and did as her sister asked, taking her in and keeping a watchful eye on the then struggling Virginia.

Saving lives and restoring happiness and safety to those who had entered their space, made them sisters entwined for life. Felicity offered legal advice to those who needed it – she did her bit to rectify women's issues.

She observed Virginia's joy.

'I was wrong about her, you know. Virginia certainly stepped up, thanks to you and Grace.'

'She did it on her own, Felicity – she was wired to make a success of her life. Hard work and passion will bring any one through tough times.'

'Amen to that!' Felicity said.

Bit by bit the softening of Felicity grew. The smile within was hard to conceal. Time created change with every life experience encountered.

Felicity looked across at Grace, 'And our next bride to be is positively glowing. Hard to believe you had a major house move yesterday. You Sharvin women are unbelievable in what you are capable of doing.' Grace lapped up this once in a lifetime praise from Felicity.

'Thank you, Felicity. I am looking forward to the gathering at the house.'

'That's a huge, positive shift, sis. We are all looking forward to you and Keefe becoming one.'

'Now, don't expect any party tricks from me! No tabletop dancing if that's what you're thinking!

'Tabletop dancing!' I am mortally wounded!' Patience laughed knowing that there were many occasions when she embarrassed her sister with her raucous laughter, and at times inappropriate comments that had Grace blushing to the roots of her curly brown hair.

Grace had accepted that Felicity's interference during their Melbourne getaway, almost two years ago, came from the seat of fear and concern for her wellbeing. The transience of life left her questioning who she was and how she presented to the world, after Alf's passing. The impermanence of life had somehow settled her. There was a still, peaceful glow in her aura.

She squeezed Felicity's arm.

'You are so grounded, and confident. I want to be in that space too.'

Felicity hugged Grace and whispered in her ear.

'You are there, Gracie.' It was the first time she referred to Grace as 'Gracie,' including her in sisterly acceptance.

Carlos bounded up to Grace, calling out on top of his voice.

'Mama, mama, look what I found!'

Encased in his little hands, he held a bonbonniere, a crocheted swan with a tiny basket of nuts and sweets tied to its back. Diane looked up from her conversation with Andrew, smiled and nodded at Grace, pleased that Carlos turned to her first as the mother he needed. His rapid transition was due in part to her affectionate nature, and the sense of safety she brought to his world. Patience was equally pleased that her sister was able to embrace Keefe's love child with compassion and maturity. Grace's love for Keefe had finally rested her past demons.

Aileen stayed in the background, watching the life that Grace and Keefe were entering. Mam would have been the happiest woman in Ireland if she was alive to witness the coming together of families who sacrificed so much to be held in shared love. The genetic connection was immaterial, it was not that blood is thicker than water that matters, it was people like Andrew, Diane, Virginia, Felicity and Keefe who made them an extended family.

The circle was expanding with a missing link returning to their lives. Anton Wessels was on his way.

A WEEK later as South African Airways touched down in Sydney, Grace felt jittery standing alone in arrivals, waiting for Anton Wessels to appear. Patience persuaded her to meet Anton alone to break the ice before they got to her place for lunch. She reminded herself that she had to be friendly, she had to avoid staring in disdain at his khaki gear. She scanned the faces coming out the exit door, but nobody familiar was in sight. Family and friends reunited in tears and laughter, how was she to react to Anton?

Then a tall, lanky man with a ruddy complexion from being outdoors too much, locked eyes with her and walked up to her with a broad smile.

'Grace, it's you. Geez, you look the same as ever. How are you?'

His voice was unchanged, his eyes held the same curiosity of the young, awkward man she remembered. Criss-crossed lines around his eyes added to the appearance of one who seemed to have collided with life's struggles. She blushed thinking it might have been obvious that she did not recognise him. His long arms were leaner with age, no longer with the curly golden hairs that glinted in the sun – now they were white, the glint stolen by time.

'Anton! Lovely to see you,' she said with forced enthusiasm, 'how was your flight?'

'I'm a little tired, ja, it's a long flight getting here.'

He had never left the country before so traveling from South Africa to Australia was a shock to his system.

'We have so much catching up to do. Would you like a cup of coffee before we go home to Patience?'

'Ja, thank you, that will be good, Grace.'

She was surprised that she enjoyed the sound of his accent with the hard 'r' sound in her name. *Grrrace* had a charm in the deliberate pronunciation. Her need to be outdoors, close to water, led to her suggestion that they have a cuppa at Brighton Bay, her favourite tranquil place.

'This is lovely, thank you, Grace. I felt really cooped up on the flight. I am a restless bugger, you know, and had to be sitting at the window seat! I did not want to disturb the people seated next to me with getting up all the time. The old knees are stiff!' He laughed, comfortable not to hold back anything from her.

'Yes, I know how you preferred being outdoors at the wood-yard and not stuck in the office. It gets really warm here in summer, this morning is passing cool weather, trust me.'

'I will be right at home then. Tell me what you sisters have been getting up to here in Australia?'

The honest bluntness of his question had good intention. She had not prepared Keefe to expect this from Anton.

'Goodness, where do I begin? It's better I tell you all about our lives, so that Patience is present when you give us your news about life in the old country.'

Time evaporated between them. Grace recalled the early days in Australia and the untimely death of her mother in a car crash. She was careful not to add in her relapse regarding Boetie Arendse. The time was not right. She saw a cloud of sadness pass over his face when she mentioned Varuna's death.

'Your mother wrote to me for several years, then with all the postal strikes, her letters never turned up. What a wonderful mother you both had. There's no one I can think of that has her caring ways. Ag, the good always go early, my Oupa used to say.'

They arrived at Patience's home, two hours later. Ajax and Sprite bounded out when they picked up Grace's scent and went into a barking frenzy when Anton got out the car.

Patience shouted above the barking, 'Welcome, welkom, Anton, kom binne.' She slipped into Afrikaans, and apologised for the dogs' bad behaviour, as she shooed them off to the backyard.

'Thank you, Patience. At least you know they will protect you. My word, what's with the water here? You, too, look like time has not touched you.'

'You are too generous, kind sir!' Patience giggled.

Patience quizzed Grace, while Anton took a shower to ease his aching joints, on what it was like seeing him after all these years. Grace said she now appreciated why her mother adored Anton. He was a gentle, polite, good soul. They spent the afternoon talking about South African politics, and what had changed in recent years. He was happy to share intimate details of his life. He met and married a woman who he thought would be his life partner, but the marriage did not survive more than a year. He was thankful they did not have children. Patience caught the look he gave Grace, but he was a gentleman as he always was, and kept his secret feelings to himself.

He went on to tell them about his incident at the woodyard. The security company called him one Sunday morning to inform him that the alarm had been set off. He went over to investigate what had happened and walked into a robbery in operation in the main office. He was gunned down and left for dead as the thieves ran off with a haul of cash from the safe. An hour later an alarm response vehicle came out when he could not be reached by telephone. He had two major surgeries thereafter and had an artificial limb after a leg amputation. Grace and Patience listened in shock. He finally said his trip to Australia was to see them in person and hand over the profit from the sale of the woodyard. His injury had slowed him down, he had to give up the business to protect his health and safety. Crime was still an issue and he was not strong enough to defend himself.

Patience shivered when she thought about Petros Sibaya and the brutal loss of his life in saving her. For all their longing for the loss of their mothers, they were indeed blessed to have so many people, Anton included, who put them first.

Varuna maintained that friends held them together through tough times when family found delight in hurling stones at them.

31

NEW FAMILY

A s Grace wanted, so it was.

A small gathering of close friends and family made her wedding reception an easy social event. With Carlos sitting between them, the Daly's united as one.

Patience, and Aileen, delivered a speech on each of their siblings as sisters that admired them. Patience was under strict instruction not to heap praise on her sister, to keep it simple, exact, with no fluff and hidden secrets.

'There is so much to say about my sister, but her humble soul implored me to say as little as possible. When Grace asks, I have to obey.' Patience shared this intimate side of her sister with Aileen.

'Aye, I can see Grace saying that. We must honour their wishes. Keefe, between you and me, asked me to say that his life was not complete until he met Grace. That's a huge public revelation, for him, I always thought he didn't have a romantic bone in his body. Grace has the magical touch, I suppose.'

Shared family joviality drew the Sharvin and Daly clan closer, a small clan they were too. Diane melted into this close-knit celebration, loving being included like she was always there. Andrew

read out a message from Nina Holstead who could not attend
with a newborn baby and little Flynn, a proud brother to his new
sister, who was down with the chickenpox. Andrew winked at
Grace and cleared his throat.

'Before I read out Nina Holstead's message, I have to share an
observation,' he turned around to look at Grace. She flinched,
hoping Andrew was not going to embarrass her. 'When Grace
returned from the conference in Amsterdam, she had a glow I
had not seen before. At first, I thought it was because she was
happy to see me,' he joked, 'but soon I learnt that the dashing Dr
Daly had stolen her heart.' Grace shook her head, smiling, as
heat rose to the tips of her ears. He continued with Nina's
message.

*Greetings from Amsterdam, lovebirds! I hope you are having a ball!
Have a dance for me this afternoon! Where shall I begin, I don't know
if I should call you Drs Daly or Dr Sharvin and Dr Daly! My dear
Grace and Keefe, I could not be happier for you. I felt the connection
between you from the first introduction, you two were destined for each
other. Grace, you have made our world warmer and Keefe's life happier
than he has ever been. Life's blessings, darlings. My Flynn is excited to
meet your Carlos someday, hopefully soon, so we too, can celebrate
your union with you.*

When Carlos heard his name uttered, he ran up to Andrew
and grabbed him around the legs. His loving nature was infec-
tious. Andrew lifted him into his arms and handed the microphone to Anton Wessels to propose a toast to the couple.

Anton, dressed in a dark blue suit, pale blue shirt and bow tie,
looked rugged and handsome. His lanky figure, more
pronounced in his dark suit, made him the tallest person in the
room. Grace was glad the vision she had of him in khaki shorts
and knee-high brown socks was no longer imprinted in her
memory. He made sure he included that Keefe was indeed a
lucky man. His appreciative look at Grace had Patience making a
note to remind her sister about the many loving male eyes, and

broken hearts she had around her when she vowed her commitment to Keefe.

The afternoon slipped into an evening of great merriment. The menu was a touch of Varuna's celebrated signature chicken curry, and a taste of Ireland with oysters for entrees and lamb and potatoes, mam's Sunday staple meal in the Daly home. Keefe sat close to Grace, holding her hand, rolling the simple gold wedding band around her finger as he whispered, 'Thank you, mo ghrá, thank you...' She squeezed his hand, they both had much to be thankful for, and she acknowledged that her mother would have been proud that she had the courage to open to love, and a life with a man like Keefe.

She walked around to greet her guests, sharing an intimate chat with each person in this close gathering. Patience brushed up against her, unable to resist a tease, whispering, 'Three men under one roof and all in love with you, shame on you!' She walked away not waiting for Grace's retort. The genial manner between the sisters was a privilege they shared as being raised by mothers who told them that life was too precious for spats and unhappiness.

Keefe noted across the room, that Andrew and Diane were lost in conversation. He whispered to Grace to look over at their table. Nothing existed for them in that moment. He looked at her with bright, eager eyes, she looked away, wanting to make eye contact but unsure if she should. Grace saw the seduction playing out before her, her pulse raced a little faster. Was it with disappointment that she missed what might have been a great love with Andrew? The man of her future sat in devotion beside her, yet her self-elected lost chance told a different story. Age and position dictated her actions. She looked away, ashamed of what she was feeling. She leaned against Keefe, fearful that Andrew would sink into the background of her life with his obvious interest in Diane, and guilt for her tinge of jealousy.

Soon after the celebrations, Grace's domestic life settled.

Patience continued to throw herself into her work and Anton Wessels left for Perth for a reunion with old school friends. He promised to return soon. Virginia took a short honeymoon in Tasmania, leaving Patience to run the SHSO office. Being at the office alone felt like she had returned to a previous life. So much had transpired since Akanya's passing. She ploughed through her emails when she saw Azmil's name pop up in her mailbox.

Sister Patience,

I hope all went well with your dear sister's wedding. What a wonderful time of celebration it must have been. The coming together of families is to be cherished. On this end, although we are still saddened by Akbar baba's disappearance, we have accepted that life must go on. Maa Zenab, in fact, insists that we move on with our life plans. She will run the Well Study Centre with Maimoona, from the house, with due diligence to avoid compromising the Mission in any way. Akbar's daughters and I will arrive in Australia at the end of the month. We are happy to advise that we have accepted your offer of accommodation until we find a place of our own. I have applied for a position at the university there and have had one online interview and there will be another when I come over to finalise the position. I am hoping all goes well with that. I do want to assist you with your SHSO, if you don't mind having me around for some of the chores that arise. I will be in touch until I arrive there. For now, sister, keep well, and thank you for all you are doing for us. Your grateful, humble friend, Azmil

EXCITEMENT FILLED HER WORLD, she had the promise of having people around her. She loved the buzz of chatting and learning from those she encountered. Now that Virginia and Grace were happily married, she had to engage in activities that prevented social isolation and loneliness. She was now third in line in the hierarchy to Grace's affection. She hoped Azmil would be granted permanency in the position at the university to ensure he was around for an extended period. She wanted to know more about him. The one thing that lingered, was whether he had abandoned the need to search for his father's family, or perhaps he was giving his thanks to Akbar first, by ensuring his daughters were happy and settled in Australia, before he moved on.

Patience committed to making frequent trips to Melbourne, to help ease Felicity's loneliness of widowhood. Aileen was a friend she could cultivate as a dinner and movie mate. She stared out the office window, watching the dense Sydney traffic snaking its way around the city. The simplicity of India was a constant yearning as she contemplated where Hiyana and Deepak were in their early love complications. Text messages and emails were brief and did not include matters of the heart. These distractions made it difficult to focus on work. She made a cup of coffee and clicked on the childhood videos she had stored on her desktop computer. Mama Varuna, Mama Elsie and Mr Sharvin, the father figure she grew up with for a brief time, smiled and laughed around the Christmas tree as she and Grace opened their presents. She stared at the screen for over an hour as a lifetime of memories rushed back across time and space to light her heart in warm remembrance.

In the solitude of the SHSO office, the floodgates gave vent to her emotions. It was not so much the lost childhood that she mourned, but the celebrated childhood that made her nostalgic. She would buy back one day if she could. Sniffing back tears, she stared at herself in the bathroom mirror, 'I am going to be fine, you better believe it, girrrl!' This brought on another bout of tears, she washed her face, looked at herself again, and held up a scolding finger, 'Stop it, Patience, pull yourself together!'

She returned to her desk, opened a box of chocolates that Virginia left for her sugar cravings, and worked through the paperwork for a new safe house in the Northern Territory. She studied the profiles of the women who would be placed there, her pain was nothing compared to what the new recruits had suffered that warranted being placed in a safe house.

That night, she was in a better space, she had Sprite and Ajax lying on the couch next to her as she read another chapter from Nelson Mandela's *Long Walk to Freedom.*

32

UNDENIABLE CALLING

A zmil was due to arrive in Australia in two weeks. He needed validation for the value he had to offer in educational circles. Her prayer was for him to see his own worth. She was determined to help him believe this. Diane returned to Spain, secure in the knowledge that Carlos was happy and settled with Keefe and Grace. Aileen doted on Carlos and threw herself into the role of loving aunt. Patience, shared the role of aunt with Aileen, stepping in only when it was necessary, to avoid being pushy. Patience's interactions with Carlos involved quality time with Sprite and Ajax. The rocky changes in their lives appeared to be gliding along with a cool breeze on their backs and no sign of clouds ahead.

Virginia returned to work, and the SHSO office moved along like a well oiled machine, the safe house in the Northern Territory was set up and Patience traveled over to welcome the ladies and settle them in.

Australia hummed with domesticity while India remained unsettled. After a lengthy conversation with Ojala, Patience penned a letter to Masuyo, to find a way around the situation there. Xandria had returned to New York to be briefed on her next assignment.

Dear Masuyo,

Truth, Understanding, and Compassion Greetings.

I hope you and Zuri are well. I am writing to you after concerns were raised by Ojala at the Panna Centre. I am only able to offer verbal advice which I don't believe is serving any good with the issues at hand there. While there is positive feedback from Pakistan with the work Judd and Alexis did to ease the family back to work, I'm afraid India needs intervention.

What are your thoughts on how this matter can be resolved? I do believe that the advice I offer should be in consultation with you, as Ojala has indicated that the Panna Centre is now exclusively the organisation's project, no longer an affiliate, as it had been under Akanya's leadership. I have a fondness for the young team there and am saddened to see them struggle in their hope to achieve what was her dream for the future of the centre.

Hoping for further news on this from you, and happy to take advice to pass to the team there. I also look forward to someday visiting you in New York. Stay well. Regards, Patience Sharvin.

WITH VIRGINIA BACK in the office full-time, Patience carved out time for a few days in Melbourne with Felicity. She had neglected her friend by being in India during Alf's passing and the busy time with all that happened in Grace's world, since her return to Sydney. Virginia urged her to take time off to see her friend to give her peace of mind that Felicity was coping after Alf's death.

She packed a small getaway bag, tossing aside her Sydney summer wear for warmer clothes for the chilly two days in Melbourne. She arrived on Felicity's doorstep at 11 o' clock, on a Saturday morning. Her usual expectation of seeing a smiling Felicity at the door was instead met with the vision of a man of senior years in black pants and a long-sleeved white shirt. For

one horrific minute Patience believed that Felicity had taken up
with another older man, as a rebound to her grief over Alf. She
pulled back her wayward thoughts to be in the moment when the
man said, 'Ms Patience, Ms Felicity will be down in a moment.
Please take a seat in the sitting room. Would Ms Patience like
some coffee?' She panicked thinking how uncanny that this was
almost like the set of an episode of *Downton Abbey*. What's with
the Ms Patience, Ms Felicity stuff and who says sitting room? His
exceedingly good manners, and polished English accent, ensured
she returned his hospitable politeness.

'Thank you, er... coffee will be good.' He immediately added,
'Morton,' 'sorry Ms Patience, that was remiss of me not to introduce myself.'

Morton? He could well be Carson down to his height,
haircut and incline of the head. She was relieved when Felicity's footsteps clicked in the hallway and then she saw her
friend's wan face. She was pale without a shred of make up. A
thinner body and absence of her usual smiling face made her a
stranger in that moment. Somehow, she managed to conceal
her weight loss under a flowing dress at Grace's wedding
reception.

'Felicity!' She stood up and hugged her friend, whispering in
her ear, 'who is this Morton character? Have you started up with
someone else?'

She felt Felicity flinch and pulled away. Morton was at the
door with a silver tray with coffee and biscuits for two. Patience
died with embarrassment, she hurriedly turned to the window to
divert her attention to the rose garden.

'Thank you, Morton, that will be all for now.'

He clicked his heels, bowed and stepped out the room in true
Carson style.

'Please tell me what's going on here, Felicity.'

'Long story, but Alf left this man in his will, to serve me, as a
butler, during my year of grieving. Whether he was serious about

this or meant it as a joke is beyond me. I cannot possibly turn him out, he is under a legal obligation as per Alf's lawyer.'

'Alf did love a sense of fun and adventure and in all honesty that is what attracted you to him, in the first place.'

'True. Apparently, there is a letter to be read after a year of his passing. I suppose, to tell Morton to leave. Who knows?'

'Men, you think you know them, and then some!' Patience laughed, 'look at what Grace had to endure, she's happy now, poor love, but it was a shock to her, finding out about the baby, the way she did. She wouldn't have it any other way now, so all's good, thankfully!'

'I am happy for Grace, Carlos is her blessing, and Keefe, he's a good man.'

Felicity had softened towards Grace. She was kind and tolerant, and Grace found her bearable after all these years.

'Well, girl, enjoy it! You are the lady of the Refalo Manor now!' Patience laughed, 'just don't ask him for a foot or back massage!'

'Oh, please be quiet, Patience, you are enjoying this a bit too much. Perhaps I will send him to vacation with Ms Patience during his summer break!' She held up her nose with an aristocratic air.

'No way! I would have to be dressed to the nines, twenty-four-seven!'

Felicity was earnest that Carson from *Downton Abbey* was her favourite character, so Morton was to be tolerated if he was a Carson replica! She explained that it might be Alf's way in getting back at her for insisting she should not be disturbed during the Sunday night screenings of the show. Patience added that perhaps Alf, who was possessive of Felicity, did not want her casting her eye on any man, and hence saddled her with a butler to distract her.

'There is no way that I want to take up with another man. I

found love, had marriage and quite frankly nobody could ever fill Alf's shoes.'

Patience felt the nostalgia of her own lost chance with Petros Sibaya flare up with that comment, the man who laid his life down for her. Try as she might, she could not move beyond that thought.

Patience was the only person allowed liberty of thought and fun at Felicity's expense. They rekindled their connection for what they loved and loathed until Felicity asked about the Mission. Patience voiced what she felt regarding the urge to return to India to assist Ojala. She revealed that she had promised Masuyo that she would spend three months at a time in Panna until the leadership there was secure and confident. She added that Ming was tied down in her new relationship and the work at her school, so that left her to assist with this dilemma.

'Gee, that will be a lot of traveling for you. How will you manage with the demands that are increasing with the SHSO?'

'It will be, but three months will pass quickly, and I can pick up when I return. I intend working online with Virginia from there. The thing I dread now, is telling Grace. I'm not sure how she will react.'

'Your passion on this, tells me that Grace will understand. She is in a different headspace now compared to the time of our Melbourne getaway. I see her strength and resilience.'

'Phew it's a relief that you are aware of this! I don't notice these changes in her, and expect her anxiety to sky-rocket every time I leave the country.'

Morton stayed in the background that weekend, serving them endless cups of coffee during the day, and preparing the meals Felicity requested, or driving them out for dinner and returning to drive them back home after they had downed too many glasses of wine. The weekend was what they both needed, to release past tension as they prepared for the next chapter in their lives.

Back in Sydney the conversation was not as easy as Felicity predicted.

'The Mission is a massive organisation, surely there are other people that can step in to help out at struggling centres. Why does it always have to be you?'

Patience had to stop Grace believing she was abandoning her because she had embarked on her new life.

'Yes, it is a massive organisation, but it's the emotional connection I have with the young people that I believe will speed up getting them to take over the reins, without too much resistance.'

'I have to ask – are you exercising your right to free will, or is Masuyo putting pressure on you to do these three monthly stints in India?'

'Free will, exclusively my decision to do so. I opted for the time frame so I don't miss out on Carlos' growing up, and I need to be around my sister and brother-in-law. It's so good seeing our family grow, Gracie!'

Grace frowned throughout their conversation, until she finally melted and accepted that she could not determine nor insist on what Patience did with her life. She had to relinquish her older sister demands. They had to allow each other to grow in their own light, that is what both their mothers modeled and expected of them. Their love for each other was unmovable, they wanted the best for each other. As Grace's attitude eased, the light-hearted side of their relationship emerged.

'Hey, I just remembered. You might still have a chance with that deputy something of police there.'

Patience looked at Grace like she had gone quite mad, 'You mean, Manik Lal? Never! He is a good friend. I have told you this before. I have no intention of finding a husband, so forget that thought!'

'Who said husband, eh? Just some romance would be good for you. Time will tell!' Grace giggled.

Patience was tempted to tease back that Grace had left part of her heart with Andrew and thought better of it. Her sister was a little jealous that Andrew had cast an admiring glance in Diane's direction – a glance that was reserved for her all these years. He was going over to Spain for two weeks in July, something she had not quite come to terms with yet.

WHAT CHANGE MAY COME IS as inevitable as night becomes day, spring turns to summer, and a storm disturbs a sunny, cloudless day. And so, the path of life veers and meanders, finding new beginnings or refreshing old ways. Nothing remains the same, except the love and respect Grace and Patience share.

The End

The Web of our Life is of a Mingled Yarn, Good and Ill Together

~ ALL'S WELL THAT ENDS WELL ~ *William Shakespeare*